Irish Thunder

by

LoLo Paige

The Wandering Hearts Series

Irish Thunder

Cover Art by *Diana Carlile*

The Wild Rose Press, Inc.
PO Box 708
Adams Basin, NY 14410-0708
Visit us at www.thewildrosepress.com

Publishing History
First Edition, 2024
Trade Paperback ISBN 978-1-5092-5084-4
Digital ISBN 978-1-5092-5085-1

Wandering Hearts Traveling Romance
Published in the United States of America

The stage changed to an icy blue, displaying Killian's white shirt with his sleeves rolled up on his forearms. His white pants fluoresced when he strolled out with his acoustic twelve-string.

A loud intake of breath met his appearance onstage. His head swiveled to the source, and he was pleased to find it was Riley. The look on her face was priceless. He preferred to consider it a look of lust.

Does she think I'm sexy? Grand...I can deliver sexy.

He lowered himself onto the tall stool and positioned the standing mic. In his sensual, come-do-me voice, he drawled, "Are we having a good time?"

His peppery gaze shot to Riley, who gave him a closed-mouth smile as whoops and hollers in the audience responded enthusiastically. "I can't hear you, ladies. I said..." He moaned an exhale into the mic as if having sex with it. "Are we having a *good* time?"

The audience clamored with hoots and hollers. "We love you, Killian!"

He milked it, loving the build of anticipation before delivering what they wanted.

A woman's voice hollered, "Take your shirt off!"

A large white thong landed on the stage in front of him. Laughter followed as he bent to retrieve it and held it high. "Someone lost this. Will the owner please come forward to claim it?"

Two older women trotted down the aisle, racing each other to the stage.

Killian tossed the thong to them, and they engaged in a tug-of-war, ripping the bloody thing in half. Killian bugged his eyes out and made an oh with his mouth. The audience ate it up, laughing and applauding. The ladies each held up their half and returned to their seats, triumphant.

Praise

LoLo's first book published by The Wild Rose Press, "Hello Spain, Goodbye Heart," won the 2019 Romance Writers of America Tara Contest. Her contemporary romance novels have garnered awards for best romance, including the Next Generation Indie Award, an Eric Hoffer, an Indie B.R.A.G. Medallion, and a Kindle Book Award. LoLo's romances about wildland firefighting have been featured in Publishers Weekly, and her true story about escaping a runaway wildfire won a 2016 Alaska Press Club award. "Alaska Spark" ranked No. 1 on Amazon Bestseller Lists in global markets, including the U.S., Canada, and Australia.

NYT bestselling author Kat Martin says, "The strong sexy women and smoking hot men who fight wildfires are written by a lady who knows, from personal experience. Fiery page-turning reads."

Dedication

For Mervin
The first person I'll visit when
I figure out how to time travel

Acknowledgments

I'm grateful to The Wild Rose Press for publishing my book, and special thanks go to my editor, Jacki Hayes, who helped me brainstorm ideas to deepen and improve the story. And thanks to Heather You for her early review and edit to help me get this story ready for submission. And finally, a huge thank you to M. Culler and Indra Devi for thoughtful reviews of my different cultures.

Chapter 1

Riley

Riley Sullivan glanced at the imposing wall clock for the hundredth time in as many minutes. The stupid thing taunted her. It was relentless: *Tick. Tick. Tick. Tick.*

The gloomy afternoon in her tenth-floor office dragged on, torturing her with monotony. She plugged away at her most exciting technical writing manual to date—*How to Assemble a Triple and Quad Rail System for Your Home.*

Who wouldn't be excited about this? Riley assured herself that she saved thousands, if not millions, of marriages by writing each intricate detail of assembling light bar fixtures for home lighting. The same way GPS navigation phone apps saved marriages with their life-saving directions on how to get to the nearest superstore for those emergency tampons.

No way would anyone blame the technical writer on her watch, by golly. This alone motivated her to be precise when writing her technical manuals. She'd watched the videos and studied photos of how the furniture was put together until her head spun.

Riley heaved out a sigh, tapped her bug-eyed glasses higher on her nose, and leaned back in her chair. She tucked a chestnut brown tendril behind her ear that had escaped her bun. Her smart phone lit with a text from

Zippy Antinoli, nagging her for the thousandth time about going out tonight.

"Already told you, I'm too tired to go out on a weeknight," Riley muttered, dancing her thumbs on her phone.

—*No, for the trazillionth time!*—

As soon as she hit 'send,' her phone sounded. With a disgruntled noise, she put the phone to her ear and fixated on the blinking cursor on her computer screen.

"I said no!" Riley shouted into her phone.

"All right already, no need to get snarky," drawled her best friend in a surly tone. A pop top opened on a soda can. Zippy subsisted on caffeinated drinks, which Riley figured was the reason for her super energetic personality. She couldn't sit still if her life depended on it. Riley could hardly keep up with her hyper friend who talked even faster than she moved.

"You haven't been out with us girls in a long time. I'm tired of your lame excuses. You didn't come out with us last weekend. Every one of us hooked up with a guy. Had you been with us, you would have too."

"Stop making sure I hook up with people. I'm not about that right now," Riley grumbled. "And I'm not gorgeous like you and your friends. I would have wound up alone again as usual to scrounge my way home."

"Don't be ridiculous. What happened to that cutie you were with? What was his name—oh yeah, Derek? You went home with him the weekend before last. You never told me what happened."

"We had meaningless, mechanical sex. That's what happened. When he got to know me, I never saw him again. I'm too boring."

"Oh stop! Riley, you're pushing thirty. You've got

to get back out there." Zippy had a way of inevitably persuading her to do things.

"I'm fed up with the dating games. Tired of pretending to be interesting when I'm not. I'm not going to the bars anymore, Zip. I'm done. No good ever comes from a one-night bar hook-up. Not for me, anyway."

Silence on Zippy's end, which was unusual. Normally, she sucked air from a room with her effervescent chatter.

"Okay," she said. "I'll let you off the hook for tonight. But that's it. From now on, you'll try harder."

"Don't waste your time, Zip. I've dug myself in."

"Still having dreams about hot Jungle Man?" asked Zippy.

"Had one a few days ago. Same as usual. I'm standing on top of a ginormous rock, and ripped Jungle Man runs up the big stone steps. He plants a kiss on me that would dissolve a thong off a stripper."

Zippy chortled, and Riley warmed at her musical laugh.

"You've never said what happens after the kiss. Does he do you, or do you reach under his loincloth?" Zippy waited expectantly.

Riley laughed and glanced at the clock. "I'll check that out in my next dream. Until then, you must live in suspense. Got to go, Zip. It's past quitting time."

"All right. I love you, despite you being a pain in the tush sometimes."

"I know. Love you too." Riley ended the call and shoved her phone into her purse. She shut down her computer and gathered her stuff to go home.

Michael, her anal-retentive boss with the million-dollar smile, stuck his head in the door. "Have you finished the LIKEA contract yet? The furniture manufacturer must have their manual written by the end of this week."

Riley flicked her eyes at her boss, then to her monitor. "I'll finish it on time," she said in a dull monotone.

Why did he resemble a movie star with his perfect, wavy hair and the fantastic body bulging through his tight-fitting sweaters? She felt inadequate around him, as if she didn't measure up. It didn't help when each day he'd give her looks of disapproval, which she construed as him judging her.

I don't care. He isn't paying me to look good, he's paying me to do whatever technical writing he landed contracts for.

She'd stopped wearing makeup. Didn't do any good, anyway. She'd taken to tossing her curly brown tresses into a tight bun at the back of her head. It was all she could do to put one foot in front of the other each day, let alone dress and go to work. Nothing ever changed. She wanted a break from monotony, but she wasn't sure how to make the changes, with lethargy as her constant companion.

Riley took the elevator to the basement garage, where she tapped her key fob and her Toyota chirped back. *At least my car loves me.*

She exited the garage, and a steady rain slapped her windshield. Her phone sounded as she switched on her wipers. Mom calling. Chewing her lip, she debated. May as well get it over with. She answered. "Hi, Mom."

"How was work today?"

"The usual. Writing overly complicated and dull directions to simplify the intricate process of assembling bookshelves or lighting fixtures."

"Oh, good, honey. Anything else of interest?"

"I also wrote how to assemble a drone."

"A what? Oh. Yes, but why are you working with male honeybees? Well, good, sweetie. Everyone should know drones help make baby bees."

Riley left it alone. "Uh-huh." She waited for the inevitable and her clueless mom didn't disappoint.

"Why don't you come home this weekend? It's not healthy for you to be alone so much."

"I'm not alone. Zippy comes over all the time," she lied. "I'm spent from the week, Mom. I'll come another weekend."

"You've been saying that for three months. Spokane isn't far from Seattle, you know."

"I know, Mom. But I have to drive over the Snoqualmie Pass. You know I hate driving in the snow."

Her mother let out a disappointing sigh. "How about we come for a visit? Your dad needs to get out of the house."

Riley scrambled for another excuse. "Have a ton of laundry and cleaning to do this weekend, and I have to work overtime to finish my writing contract." She hoped enough excuses would dissuade her mother.

"All right. We haven't seen you in a long time. Thought it'd be nice to spend a few days together. We could take you to dinner at the top of the Space Needle. I love how the restaurant moves around in circles. The view is so pretty."

"Remember the last time you set your purse on the window shelf and we went around without it?" Riley reminded her.

"But I got it back on the second trip."

"Mm-hm. You were lucky no one took it." Riley braked for a red light, blurry through the heavy rain. "Mom, it's pouring and I'm driving. Got to go. Love you, bye." She ended the call and tossed her phone on the passenger seat. All Riley wanted was to be left alone. She didn't have the energy to deal with anyone right now.

She cranked the radio volume and merged onto the freeway with bumper-to-bumper traffic. After an hour of stop-and-go freeway fun, she pulled into the basement of her five-story apartment building and rolled into her numbered parking spot. She hurried to her apartment and once inside, tossed her purse on a chair and tugged off her raincoat.

Her TV beckoned. She grabbed the remote and channel surfed. News depressed her. She made a face and surfed for a sitcom. An emerald landscape surrounding a castle grabbed her attention. She peered at the name of it: Blackwater Castle in County Cork, Ireland. Colorful flowers abounded in a landscaped garden near the banks of a river.

Yes! The Travel Channel!

Riley stared at the beautiful scene and inserted herself into it, wishing she could mosey along the stone path. She'd weave around the ferns, stop to smell the flowers, and stand on the stone bridge with the quaint water wheel along the sleepy brook to watch the miniature waterfalls. The narrator talked about people who got married at Blackwater Castle.

Fat chance I'll ever get over to Ireland.

She'd wanted to go ever since Mom and Dad informed her of her Irish heritage. She'd never felt she belonged anywhere. Not even in her hometown of Spokane.

She wished she could visit Ireland and track down her family lineage; find some place she belonged. She'd considered signing up for a group tour but never followed through. Just because she had Irish heritage didn't mean she could afford to visit the motherland.

Riley didn't want to go alone. But the real reason was, she didn't want to put herself out there socially. Nope, she didn't welcome reminders of what she lacked—her boring personality, for one, and her looks weren't anything great either.

It was easier to stay in her safe, comfortable world at home in her apartment. She preferred losing herself in the big city as another ho-hum face in the Seattle crowd. Riley had applied for the technical writing job with Michael because it covered the expenses of her tiny, overpriced apartment.

She lived frugally. That was the real reason she didn't want to go out with Zippy and the other girls—she couldn't afford it and was too embarrassed to admit it. Zippy worked as a paralegal for a reputable law firm, and the rest of their friends had high-paying jobs.

Riley had her books and movies to keep herself company. She curled up with her soft, furry throw and clicked back to the travel channel to watch exotic places from afar. Maybe someday she'd travel overseas.

Someday, when she could afford it. And when she felt better about herself.

Chapter 2

Killian

"What do you mean, we're performing on a cruise ship?" Killian O'Sullivan howled at Rex, his manager, who'd followed him out to his blue sports car in the Golden Desert Hotel and Casino parking lot. "Why can't we stay on the Vegas strip?"

"Told you before, show production costs on the strip have skyrocketed. I've scheduled this first cruise to see if Wanderlust Travel, Inc. wants to continue our show," explained Rex in his Irish brogue.

"But I have a trip planned to Cork. You said we had a week's break." Looked like Killian's dreams of a visit to his hometown in southeast Ireland vanished along with the Vegas gig.

Rex lit a cig and blew out smoke. "You can take a wee break to go home after the cruise ends."

"Oh, cripes," sputtered Killian, pulling his sunglasses from his pocket and placing them on his tanned face. "Told you before, I get seasick. What if I puke in the middle of performing?"

"I'll get you anti-nausea pills," said Rex. "The cruise filled right away once Wanderlust Travel began advertising it. I didn't have to pay for marketing. This will be a boost for Irish Thunder."

Killian shook his head. "A boost? Taking off my

clothes while I upchuck onstage? Yeah, that'll turn the ladies on."

"Better get things wrapped up here. We're on a flight to Fort Lauderdale the week after next. Here's your share of this week's tips." Rex pressed a roll of bills into Killian's palm.

He scrutinized the roll of one-hundred-dollar bills and smiled. "Gonna miss this."

"You'll get even more tips on the boat." Rex slapped Killian's shoulder and gave it a fast shake. "You can do this, lad. It's only for a week. You can do anything for seven days."

"You said the same when we told you we didn't want to strip," said Killian with a dour look.

"And look what happened—the ladies can't get enough, and we raked in the cash. Got to run and complete the cruise contract. Get busy packing." Rex climbed into his red muscle car and cranked the engine.

Killian stared at his manager as he sped off. He let out a long sigh, longing for more control over his life. At first, handing control over to Rex seemed a great idea, so he could focus on his music. But as time wore on, the four Irish Thunder performers had less and less of a say about their show. Now they had no say. Killian missed the satisfaction of composing songs.

He brushed back his shoulder length, sun-lightened hair with his fingers and tucked it behind his ears. Leaning on his prized Mustang, he thought about how stable his life had become, staying in one performance venue for so long. How bad could it be on a cruise ship? He'd arm himself with a truckload of anti-nausea pills. On a positive note, the cast and production team had been working hard and could use this break from routine.

It was only for a week. He could stand on his head for a week.

Killian started his convertible and pointed it toward the condo he'd rented in Henderson with the other three men in the Irish Thunder group: Declan, Sean, and Willy.

He'd miss the throngs of women that were a constant draw to their singing strip show, along with the fantastic pay. He'd had his share of dating beautiful women but felt devoid of any heartfelt relationships.

When Rex had first approached the group about morphing their singing and dancing production into an Irish strip venue, all four guys had resisted. It started when their music sales had declined, and Rex drummed up the brilliant idea of shedding their clothes at the end of their shows—his genius way of 'shaking things up'.

Once Killian learned the dance choreography, taking off his clothes wasn't a big deal. He had to work out like a wild man, to grow the bulges where they counted on his chest and abdomen. He was no Mister Universe by any stretch but had managed a wee six-pack.

It shook things up all right—Irish Thunder's song and dance strip show became an overnight sensation in Las Vegas. Not only because they were Irish, which Americans crushed on, but they sexy-danced, wearing only their kilts, which became more popular with the women than their music ever was.

Unfortunately, with rising costs to stay in production on the strip, Rex suspended Irish Thunder's Vegas contract and replaced it with a cruise ship entertainment contract. As per usual, he didn't check with the group before booking it. Killian's manager was an expert at following the money trail.

Oh man, anything but a fecking cruise ship! Why do

I allow my manager control over my life? It's time to grow some balls and do what's best for me.

Killian opened the door to the condo to find Declan guzzling a beer and Willy on the phone, most likely with his girlfriend in Dublin. He headed to the fridge and pulled out a bottle of mineral water.

"Beer makes you fat, dude," said Killian as he took a pull on his bottle.

Declan ran a hand over his stubble, his dark hair pulled back in a ponytail. "We have a week off. I plan to enjoy myself before we do this cruise gig." He reached for a bag of corn chips and chomped on one. "I gave notice to the landlord we'd be gone for a while."

"When does everyone fly to Florida?" asked Killian, sinking into his favorite chair.

"Willy Boy leaves tomorrow. He plans to spend time with his woman before the cruise." Declan grinned. "I'm not leaving until I say goodbye to the lovelies I'll be missing. Sean is—well, Sean. He never knows what he's doing until he does it."

Killian chuckled at the reference to their fourth group member. Sean the rebel hated being told what to do and continually teetered on the edge of breaking his entertainment contract—mainly because he couldn't keep his homeboy in his pants. None of the men hurt for female companionship, but Killian had tired of the shallow, fake personalities their industry attracted.

Lately he'd been restless, wishing he could meet someone honest and sincere—a woman who wasn't after his money, ripped physique, and good looks. Not likely, if he stayed in this business.

"Does Mariah know?" asked Killian.

Declan rolled his eyes. "She couldn't pack fast

enough. Took the first flight to Florida. With any luck, she'll find another production to terrorize."

Killian laughed and shot his friend a twisted smile. "And good riddance."

"I can tell it breaks your heart, eh, Kils?" teased Declan. The Irish Thunder men secretly regarded Mariah Perez as a joke, as she moved from one to the next, in hopes of getting one to marry her. They'd placed bets on who'd become her next victim.

Mariah joined the production last year when Rex decided he wanted female soloists and Irish troupe dancers to balance things for the boyfriends and husbands that women dragged to their shows. Mariah had sprung from the gate, lusting for Killian first, and — like an idiot—he fell for her charms and slept with her. He severed the relationship cord when he realized Mariah was only after his fame and money.

Performing didn't fulfill Killian the way it used to when he first formed the Irish rock band in Dublin seven long years ago. They'd hired Rex from Galway as their manager, and he'd gotten them into the big time— provided they blended their rock with Irish music for global appeal. Rex had the group focus on singing and harmonizing instead of playing their instruments.

Time to pack for the cruise. He rose and wandered around his bedroom. It was a good thing Killian didn't get attached to possessions. He learned early on the fewer items he had, the easier it was to travel when they'd toured before landing the Vegas gig.

Hopefully, he'd get time to relax and play his guitar—write songs as he used to do. There was never time to do what he loved. After performing each night, he was too knackered for anything except to rest up and prepare for the next physically demanding performance.

Killian hoped for calm seas. The last thing he wanted was to spend the cruise curled around a bucket. He hoped Rex was being honest in saying he'd signed a contract for this gig to be a one-time thing.

The last thing Killian wanted was to spend the rest of his performance life on the high seas.

Chapter 3

Riley

Riley groaned at the relentless pounding on her apartment door. "All right, all right, I'm coming!"

Though it was Saturday afternoon, she'd stayed in her tee shirt and flannel PJs. She shuffled to the door in her golden retriever puppy slippers and unlocked the two bolts and undid the chain.

She swung it open to see Zippy holding two cardboard espresso go-cups and a sack from Riley's favorite neighborhood bakery.

"Why haven't you answered your phone? I've been calling and calling. Take this," ordered Zippy, offering Riley one of the hot coffee cups with the white lid and a monkey-face sticker over the sippy hole. Zippy breezed past her and plonked her pile of keys and purse on the coffee table, cluttered with stacks of books and magazines.

"You won't believe this," announced Zippy, waving her coffee cup. "Wait until you see how incredible this is. I'm busting!" Her large brown eyes glittered with excitement.

Riley plucked off the tiny paper monkey sticker and sipped her hot latte, waiting for Zippy to spill her news.

"Aren't you going to ask me what is so flipping amazing?" Zippy tossed back her thick, bottle-blonde hair. She rummaged through her purse, retrieved her phone, and held it so close to Riley's face that Riley's eyes crossed.

"Feast your peepers on *this!*"

Riley put on her bug-eyed glasses and squinted. "You won a drawing for what?"

Zippy gurgled an exasperated noise. "Gah! A two-fer!"

Riley shrugged. "A two for one coffee? Cool, congratulations."

Zippy swiped her phone and held it out. "I won a two for one Caribbean cruise!" she squealed, jumping and dancing around. "I entered an online drawing a couple of months ago and forgot about it. Wanderlust Travel emailed me, and at first, I thought it was a spam scam. When I called them, they said no, it was real."

"And you believed them."

Zippy rolled her eyes. "You're such a skeptic. Yes! It's *real!*"

Riley took a moment to process Zippy's exciting news. "Wow, if it's real, that's great. I'm excited for you."

Zippy hopped over, looking down at her. "For us. You're going with me."

Possibility niggled Riley. "You want me to go? Seriously?"

Zippy scowled. "Who else would I ask to go?"

"The current hot squeeze you're dating?"

Zippy gave her a withering look. "Hardly." She sat next to Riley. "I haven't told you the best part."

"Which is?" Riley wondered how much better the news could be.

"It's an Irish Thunder cruise in the Caribbean!"

Riley gave her a blank look. "What's that?"

"Not a what, it's a who. You don't know who Irish Thunder is?"

"Um, should I?"

"Shame on you. You're Irish. You should know Irish Thunder is the hottest male band right now. They used to play their concerts on those pledge drives for public TV, before they changed up their show and took their clothes off."

Riley scoured her brain. "You don't mean the singing Irish guys who strip in Vegas? You and I planned to go see them one time."

Zippy's face lit up like a birthday cake. "They don't play Vegas anymore. Now they do these cruises."

It became clearer to Riley what her bestie offered. "You won two trips for the price of one for a cruise—with those cute Irish guys as the entertainment?" Her jaw hung open.

Zippy grasped Riley's hands and squeezed. "I know, right? You've got to come with me."

Reality reared its ugly head. "I don't know if I can get time off work. Michael will say I can't leave until I've completed my manuals. It's what he says whenever I've asked for time off. Never mind that I have a bazillion days of unused vacation."

"You *have* to go!" Zippy shot her an urgent look. "This is a once in a lifetime opportunity. I know we'd have a blast. The cool thing is, we'd split the cost of one trip." Her chocolate stare pierced Riley. "And don't say you can't afford it. It won't get any cheaper than this for a seven-day cruise."

Riley's head filled with confusion. "I can't decide right now. Need to think about it."

"You have ten minutes to decide—starting now. We leave in two weeks." Zippy touched the time app on her phone and held it out to Riley, tapping her foot. "It's high time you take risks. Seize opportunities. You don't want to be eighty with a lifetime of regret."

Zippy's free hand snatched Riley's phone. "Call Michael right now. Do it!"

"I can't call my boss at home."

"Why? He's single but has no life. He's too busy admiring himself in the mirror and jerking off to porn."

"Come on, be nice," admonished Riley.

"I don't like the way he treats you." Zippy had nothing good to say about Riley's boss, the few times she'd met him at holiday parties and when visiting Riley's office.

"I know you don't." Riley leaned back on the couch. *How can I get all my contracts done in a week?*

It was a physical impossibility.

Zippy's phone sounded with her cheery tune of the month. "Hello, cutie." She winked at Riley and rose from the couch, moving to the window.

Riley picked up the remote and clicked through channels. The travel channel showed an Irish pub with people dancing. She muted the sound to listen to Zippy flirt with her latest one-night stand.

"Of course, I'd love to come," purred Zippy, turning to Riley and fluttering her lashes.

Riley laughed at her friend's ability to never take relationships with men seriously. She strung them along like beads on a necklace until she was ready to move on to the next. And she was gorgeous enough to pull it off without a hitch.

"Bye," said Zippy, ending her call. She tossed her

phone into her purse. "Jason wants me to go with him to his friend's engagement party tonight. I have to go find something to wear." She gathered her purse and jacket and paused.

"Talk to Michael first thing Monday. Don't ask. Tell him you're going. He holds you hostage to every stupid writing contract he gets, like Ebenezer Scrooge. The world can wait another week for you to write directions on how to assemble a bunk bed. Call me Monday after you talk to him." Zippy vanished out the door.

Riley stared after her, her brain whirling. She'd never gone on a cruise. But her lack of ability to hold her own in random social situations twisted her insides.

Glancing out at the never-ending rain beading her window, her heart thudded, and she dreaded Monday. *What's the use? Michael won't let me go, anyway.*

She shifted her gaze to the TV and unmuted it. The Irish tunes lifted her spirits, like a magic elixir. Why couldn't she be free-spirited, like Zippy? What was it that bogged her down and made her afraid?

Her blue eyes misted, blurring the TV image. Rejection. Ongoing judgment: not good enough. Not witty enough. Not pretty. Certainly not pretty.

And inevitably saying the wrong thing.

The program featuring the Irish tour had a boat ferrying cars across the River Shannon. She yearned to go, but it was impossible—too far away. Not having the means to visit places like Ireland made her sad. She stared wistfully at the images.

Riley ruminated over what Zippy had bluntly pointed out. She'd waffled around for five years within the status quo, never deviating, doing what she was told without question. Each day blended into the next; the inertia of her life heading nowhere fast.

Zippy was right. If Riley didn't seize this opportunity, it may not come around again. What's the worst that could happen if she told Michael she was going no matter what?

I could lose my job.

The idea of being unemployed terrified her. But she'd have more time to write her poetry. She glanced at the stack of journals on her table. She'd filled at least a dozen and hadn't done a thing with them. Not even entered a poetry contest or shared her poems with Zippy.

What would I gain by playing it safe like I always have?

If she didn't ask for what she wanted and stood up for herself—what then? Her status quo would continue. Sure, she'd keep her job, but she'd forever wonder what would have happened had she gone on the cruise.

Riley stood to click the TV off when a closing image caught her eye—a cruise ship sailing off in a cerulean sea. She couldn't pry her eyes from it.

"What are you waiting for?" a dreamy voice urged.

Good point. What the heck am I waiting for?

All right, she decided. She had all day Sunday to plan what she would say to Michael.

If I don't ask for what I want, I'll never forgive myself.

Chapter 4

Riley

Two weeks later.

Riley's heart raced as she scooted up the gangway to the gargantuan cruise ship, tugging her over-stuffed carry-on behind her.

"Wait up, girl!" hollered Zippy, following her. "This isn't a race, you know." She breathed hard behind Riley after hurrying to get in line to board.

Riley showed her paperwork to the uniformed crew member, who stamped it, checked her ID, and waved her onboard. She waited for Zippy, and once on the enormous cruise ship, they strode along the glittery hallways to find their stateroom.

"Where's the Calypso Deck? I want to go to the pool." Riley glanced around for a sign. "Look at all these elevators. Which one goes where?"

Zippy squinted. "I don't know. Read the signs. I can't wait to check out the spa, eight lounges and bars, and the casino."

"You gamble and I'll hang in the spa," said Riley, craning her neck. There was much to take in. The interior of the ship sparkled with gold and glitter everywhere— on the floors, the walls, the staircases, even the elevators.

"Remember, we paid extra for a balcony," said

Zippy. "You'll thank me later. I know you griped about forking over a couple hundred extra, but trust me, you'll love it."

Riley stood waiting for one of the four elevators. Each time a door opened, the elevator was full. "We'll never get on one. Let's take the stairs."

Zippy made a pained face. "No way. I'm waiting for an elevator." She stayed put, leaning on the handle of her upright carry-on.

"Suit yourself." Riley rolled her bulging bag toward an elaborate spiral staircase. She lowered her worn bag one step at a time while holding onto the curved teak railing. She eased it down another. This would take all day. She kicked herself for not waiting for an elevator.

Focused on getting her overfilled bag to the next lower step, the heel of her white sandal caught, and she lost her balance.

"Oh, no!"

Her carry-on took off without her as she gripped the railing with both hands to keep from falling. Her bag had a mind of its own, lumbering the rest of the way down the glittery spiral staircase.

She groaned as the damaged zipper separated and the bag burst open, scattering bras, undies, and the rest of her intimates for all the world to see. She shouldn't have packed it to the max. It had ripped when she'd heaved it onto the conveyor belt at SeaTac airport, and she'd crossed her fingers it would hold together.

A voice with a thick Irish accent called out. "Hello? Do these things belong to you?"

Oh great. Of course, some dude found her intimates. She squeezed her eyes closed.

"Hello? Anybody there?" A tanned face framed with

blond shoulder-length hair peered up at her as she gingerly made her way to the bottom of the stairs. Every item she'd hauled onto this ship lay displayed for everyone's amusement.

Horrified by the fiasco, Riley couldn't respond to the tall handsome man in a loose-fitting blue tee shirt and Hawaiian board shorts. He stood staring at her, oozing masculinity.

"Are these things yours?"

"Yes, they're mine!" she gasped, panic tremoring her voice. She swooped down to grab her bright pink lacy thong, but he beat her to it by snatching it and dangling the shocking pink lace from his forefinger.

"Here you go."

When she looked at his face, she found a recognizable quality about him. The corners of his mouth lifted, and Riley thought she might faint. This hunk was gorgeous—mother-flipping perfect looking. She searched for a flaw.

Must be one somewhere.

Flustered, she reached for the thong when his other hand slid into hers. "Happy to help, Miss…?" His hand warmed hers as he squeezed it.

"Uh, Riley. With an E and a Y." Her eyes flicked up to meet his chocolate ones, reflecting the gilded decor of the glittery staircase.

Mortified, she flopped down, snatched up her panties and bras, and crammed them into her busted bag.

"Riley, with an E and a Y, you're sorely in need of duct tape." He bent and folded her bag closed. "I'm happy to take this to your room for you."

"Oh, you don't have to do that," she blurted, her cheeks heating. She brushed her fingers over her hair, pulled back in her usual eye-stretching bun.

"Where's your room?" Hot Irish Guy's baby browns gleamed with interest as they fixed on her.

Her spine tingled as she took him in. "On the sixth deck."

"Oceania Deck…" He edged over to a wall sign and ran his finger down the deck list. "Let's take the elevator."

"Okay," she said faintly, her eyes feasting on six feet of eye candy.

He strode off with her carry-on under his arm, tucking it into his side as if it were a lightweight football.

Riley had little choice but to follow. By the time she caught up to him, he'd already pushed the button and the elevator door opened. They stepped in, and he pressed the Oceania Deck button. The door closed and an old couple stood smiling at them.

"On your honeymoon?" the woman asked Hot Irish Guy.

He grinned at Riley and raised his eyebrows. "Yes, and we're having a grand time," he said in his sexy Irish lilt.

"Make the most of it, you two. Time is precious." The woman smiled, her thin-lipped husband nodding in agreement.

Riley gave Hot Irish Guy a sidelong glance of disbelief, at the same time an unexpected warmth surged through her.

The door opened, and he turned to Riley. "What's your room number?"

Still reeling from his honeymoon comment, Riley raised her eyes to find him watching her. "Since you said we were on our honeymoon, shouldn't you know the room number? Come to think of it, I don't know your name, so why would I tell you my room number? For all I know, you could be a cruise ship serial killer."

His brow lifted. "You must be from New York or L.A."

"Not even close." Riley dug in her purse for the paperwork with her room number. "Fifteen thirty-two."

She peered at the numbers and arrows on the wall of a narrow corridor. "This way." Riley led off, keenly aware Hot Guy's gaze bored into her as he followed.

"You haven't told me your name," she called over her shoulder.

"Killian," he said. "With a K. And no worries. I'm not a serial killer."

"Killian, as in the beer?"

He chuckled. "Yep, like the beer."

She stopped at her room and rummaged through her purse for her key card. Finding it, she waved it over the lock and a green light blinked. She opened the stateroom door.

Zippy flew at her with a flute of bubbly. "About time you showed up! I've been waiting to toast us—" Zippy stopped short upon seeing Killian with a K follow Riley into their room.

He rested Riley's bag on a twin bed. "Anything else, Miss Riley? Happy to be your bag steward today."

"Thank you." Riley pulled a twenty from her wallet, not caring about the amount. This person had fondled her underwear, and she just wanted him to leave.

He glanced at the bill and grinned. "No need to tip me. I was happy to do it."

"You—you went to all this trouble for me," she stammered.

"You went to all this trouble for her," echoed Zippy, her eyes locked on Killian. She turned to Riley with a quizzical look. "What happened to your bag?"

Riley noted Zippy's slacked jaw as her bestie stood holding a flute of champagne.

"I tripped, the zipper broke, and my carry-on crashed down the stairs." Riley gestured at Killian. "He was kind enough to help."

"No worries. Happy to do it." He pulled out a phone and glanced at it. "Got to run. Nice meeting you ladies. Hope to see you around, Riley." Their eyes met for a moment, then Killian let himself out and closed the door.

Zippy's eyes popped. "Where the heck did you get him? He has to be the hottest guy on this ship!"

She threw back her champagne, grabbed the bottle, and poured some into another flute. She handed it to Riley. "Here's to Mr. Eye Candy! And to more like him."

"His name is Killian." Riley laughed and sucked the champagne down like a glass of cold water. "Of all people to peruse every bra and panty I own, it had to be some brawny Irish guy," she groaned.

"Consider it a stroke of luck! I'd love for him to fondle *my* underwear." Zippy blew out air. "He has a Brad Pitt vibe, don't you think? Except with longer hair and a more perfect face."

Zippy's mouth hung open in that funny way when she'd discovered something. "Hold on a second." She tapped her phone and squealed. "Know who that was? Oh my God!"

She tossed her phone to Riley. "That was Killian O'Sullivan, the uber popular lead singer of Irish Thunder. How did I not connect those dots? I'm falling down on the job!"

The stud who'd been in their room was indeed on the cover of Irish Thunder's latest music collection, *Naked Thunder*. A suit jacket and kilt decorated his fine physique, as he stood smiling with the rest of the not-so-bad-looking threesome.

Something about his familiarity alerted the hair on the back of Riley's neck. She didn't know why, nor could she pinpoint it. She'd sensed it at the bottom of the stairs when first looking into his eyes—like she already knew him. Impossible.

I've never met this man until a few minutes ago.

Riley's jaw dropped. "He's in the Irish Thunder group? Had I known, I would have bolted. He saw my flipping underwear, for gosh sakes." Her neck hairs rose so tall she could tie them in a knot.

"Most women would find that erotic."

Riley lifted her chin and sniffed. "I'm not most women."

"Apparently not." Zippy grasped Riley's arm. "Let me clue you in. Did you catch the look that Irish Thunder Boy gave you when he said he hoped to see you again?"

"He has to be nice to everyone. He's an entertainer. It's his job," Riley said dismissively, holding the phone so close she nearly went cross-eyed. "There's something familiar about him. Can't put my finger on it. I probably saw a picture of him someplace." She tossed Zippy's phone on the bed.

"I'm sure you have. *Celebrity Magazine* named Killian O'Sullivan one of the top ten sexiest men." Zippy snatched the phone, worked her thumb and forefinger, and zeroed in on the four Irish Thunder crotches. She tilted her head in a critical assessment.

"This Sean person isn't bad and seems well hung.

Wonder if he has a girlfriend."

"I'm sure he does." Riley rolled her eyes. "Geez, Zip, all you think about is sex."

Her best friend gave her a dour look. "Well, someone has to!"

Riley grinned at her friend. "There's no hope for you." She slid the glass door open and moved to their pocket-sized balcony. "Whoa, come check this out."

The massive cruise ship had pulled away from the dock, maneuvered a 360 on its center to turn around, and now glided along a water corridor toward the open Atlantic. Riley loved the sound of waves gently lapping the hull as the ship parted the water on their gateway to adventure. She couldn't wait for all the wonderful things to come.

"Don't you freaking love this?" Zippy stepped out and linked Riley's arm. They stood watching the sunset's coral reflection on the city buildings as the ship slipped out to sea.

"Glad you got us this balcony, Zip. This is worth it." Riley eyed the lifeboats lined up on the outside of a deck five levels below. She didn't want to think about needing one.

Zippy moved inside and unpacked her bag. "Here's something for you. I bought it for me, but it's too big in the chest. It'll fit you better. I told you that people dress up on these cruises." She unfolded a navy-blue cocktail dress with scattered sparkles and tossed it at Riley. "And here are silver peep-toe heels to go with it."

They conveniently wore the same size. Whenever Riley visited Zippy's much nicer apartment, she'd beeline to Zippy's closet to try on her shoes and boots, since she couldn't afford those designers on her own.

"Better hurry. Dinner is in thirty minutes. The first Irish Thunder show starts soon after in the large theater." Zippy wriggled into a low-cut red dress.

"I'm so hungry I could eat a humpback." Riley tugged off her tank top.

Zippy pointed to the tiny bathroom. "I plugged in the curling iron and set some makeup out for you to use. Take your hair out of that god-awful bun and curl the sides and your bangs. You remind me of my great-grandmother back in Sicily. Hurry, I have to curl my own hair."

Riley stepped to the mirror and noted Zippy's makeup scattered on the tiny counter next to the sink. She picked up eyeliner and mascara and applied both.

Zippy squeezed in next to her. "Scootch over. You don't know squat about applying mascara and eye shadow," she said impatiently, setting to work on Riley's eyes like that man on TV who makes painting pictures look so easy.

"There. Happy little lashes." Zippy leaned back to assess. "Here, put on this lipstick." She shoved a fuchsia shade at Riley, who dutifully did what her bestie instructed.

The women hustled out of the bathroom, wriggled toes into peep-toed heels, and grabbed their purses. As they hurried to the elevator, the image of Killian in their stateroom occupied real estate in Riley's head.

Those chocolate-truffle eyes hadn't judged her with approval or disapproval—he'd only been amused at her situation. She'd picked up good vibes from him. If he hadn't judged, she wouldn't either. She'd reign in her skepticism and keep an open mind, as Zippy had advised.

Her heart sped at the anticipation of seeing Killian onstage. If she didn't talk to him again, at least she could feast her eyes on him as he performed onstage for the rest of the cruise.

Life on the high seas was looking good.

Chapter 5

Killian

"Where've you been? Get your ass in gear," barked Rex, as Killian burst through the door of the Irish Thunder VIP suite in the ship's bow.

"I had your three-piece suits pressed before boarding, so you'd all look spiffy for opening night." He motioned at a closet, where Declan, Willy and Sean had already retrieved their suits and were busy dressing.

Rex put on his reading glasses. "Here are my notes from today's rehearsal. This stage is smaller than Vegas. A few of you missed the marks for your solos. I put glow tape on the floor to mark your spots, so Siobhan can pre-set her spotlights. Don't go rogue onstage."

Killian hummed as he zipped his creased, dark blue trousers and buckled his tan belt. His mind reverberated with Riley. Not a raving beauty, but something in her big blue eyes had intrigued him. Was it a determined independence of spirit, or a faraway look? He'd refrained from chuckling at seeing her crimson cheeks and how her soulful eyes popped behind her librarian glasses when she discovered him holding her lacy pink thong.

Killian couldn't shake the sense that he'd met her before. More than likely at one of their shows. He'd met thousands of fans.

Grinning, he congratulated himself on his creativity

in the heat of her awkward moment by offering to help.

"…and you sang flat on a few notes in your 'Shannon of Long Ago' solo. You'd better warm up," droned Rex. "Killian! Did you hear me?"

Killian snapped to the present and glanced at Sean, who winked at him with a 'here we go again' expression.

"Sure did, boss."

"Good. Now get your arses to the green room, where Siobhan will fix your hair. Wait for my 'Places' call."

"Aye-aye, Cap'n." Killian saluted Rex on his way out, tossing his tie around his neck.

The four men took the back stairs behind a partitioned-off portion of the ship for VIPS and entertainers. At this morning's rehearsal, Killian couldn't get over how large the theater was for a cruise ship. He'd read that a famous Italian movie star had designed the ship's interior. She did a classy job.

When the guys reached the green room where they'd wait to be summoned onstage, Sean stepped close to fix Killian's tie. "It's time you learned how to do this, Kils. Dress you up, can't take you anywhere."

Sean had the thickest brogue of the lot, being from Donegal. He'd also been a good friend since he and Killian had put the band together back in Dublin.

Siobhan sailed into the room. "Ready boys? We're running a wee bit late. Sit still while I doll you up," she ordered Killian. She had her hair fixings in her apron pocket and whipped out a brush to smooth out Killian's thick mass. He enjoyed her large bosom brushing him as she leaned close to work on his hair.

"You're ready for a trim, Kils. Hair's below your collar. They'll be callin' ya Celtic Woman." She winked. "Keep these blondish streaks. They work. The women love it."

Killian gave her a wicked look. "The women love it, or do *you* love it?"

She held out an electric shaver. "Sorry, you can't have me. I'm saving myself for someone who's handsome," she sniffed. "Now ditch the five o'clock shadow. This isn't a biker concert."

"Yes, ma'am." Killian knew better than to mess with Siobhan. He took the shaver and spruced up his face, as instructed.

The drums and electric guitar played, and a harp, bass, and violinist joined in to warm up the audience. Killian normally didn't get the heebie-jeebies before a show, but this was his first time performing on a ship. Though he'd taken two anti-nausea tablets, envisioning this gargantuan ship tossing around like a toy boat didn't set his mind at ease.

"Rex, can you please pre-set my acoustic guitar onstage for the Ireland tribute solo?" Playing his acoustic twelve-string calmed him. When the band first started, he'd been the drummer and played guitar. Rex hired a drummer so Killian could focus on his vocals and playing guitar.

Rex stared at him for a moment. "Remember the last time when you broke your strings? Don't let it happen again. You're playing the guitar, not your drums. This guitar is beat to shit. You need a new one."

"Can't afford a fancy one. Unless *you* buy one for me?" Killian gave him a hopeful look. "No worries, I'll go easy on the strings tonight." Truth be told, Killian had a few too many beers toward the end of their Vegas run and pounded his guitar a tad too hard.

Kenny, the leather-clad sound designer, approached

the singers with tiny wireless mics and clipped one to each of their lapels. "Sound check. Go." He pointed at each, who automatically cycled through their voice checks of one, two, three, check, while Kenny adjusted for clarity and volume.

"You're good to go, lads. Have a great show." Kenny strode out to his booth to make the technical magic that made them sound fantastic.

Siobhan pulled off her apron and put on her headphones. "Time to light this puppy. Break a leg, fellas." She scurried to her post.

Killian respected her expertise in light design. She worked magic with the computers, light gels, and filters. Siobhan dimmed the lights in the green room.

"Places, lads!" Rex stage whispered.

The four men filed out and took the stage in the dark. Killian's favorite part of the show was now, as lights came up on the drummer upstage on his own platform, pounding a haunting beat, building in volume and tempo. As the beat intensified and hit a crescendo, the lights flashed and swept up onto the four Irish Thunder performers, spread out at intervals across the stage.

Killian swaggered downstage with his cronies as the four broke out in unison to sing the first notes of a lively Irish ballad. He scanned the audience faces, their eyeglasses reflecting the stage lights. He pasted on his Irish Thunder smile as he belted from his diaphragm the way his music teacher had taught him years ago, when he sang in the church choir in Cork.

After the men finished their opening medley of three songs, the audience erupted with applause, screams, and whistles. The lights darkened and the music segued for the scene change. The group rushed offstage to shed their jackets and roll up shirt sleeves for the next medley of Irish ballads, interspersed with instrument solos. Even though Killian had done this show hundreds of times, he stepped carefully upon re-entering the dark stage. He followed the glow tape Siobhan had carefully positioned on the stage floor, to show the way to his mark.

When the lights came up and the music thundered from the massive sound system, Killian's gaze swept the audience. One face caught his rapt attention, and he wasn't sure whether it was the same woman he'd encountered on the spiral staircase. He trained his gaze on her as he sang, and when her eyes caught his, he smiled, and she beamed back at him.

Yep, that's her.

Riley Sullivan resembled nothing like she had earlier. Now, she was positively radiant. His mind raced as his autopilot thankfully kicked in and he moved around the stage with his Irish Thunder lads. Upstage on a platform, Rex stood in a kilt, waving a full-sized Irish flag. Downstage, the boys ended their Irish anthem with a stomp of their feet, along with the drum for final impact.

His mind kept coming back to Riley with an E and a Y. Something about the brown-haired woman fascinated him. She hadn't crushed on his celebrity, and he enjoyed that. He grinned, knowing what he would do.

Wait until she sees what I have in store for her.

Intermission couldn't come soon enough.

Chapter 6

Riley

During the fifteen-minute break in the middle of the show, Zippy stood. "I require a glass of wine. Want one?"

Riley held up her hand. "I've had enough with the champagne. I'll hang out here."

"I'll be right back." Zippy scooted out to the aisle where people milled around, stretching their legs.

During the first half of the show, Irish Thunder's music had impressed Riley. The men's voices were pure and charged with emotion.

Her eyes had glued to Killian, and she'd noted his confident, straight-backed posture, the mark of a professional entertainer. She wondered how many women he had on his string. A wife or a girlfriend probably pined for him somewhere. Men like him were inevitably spoken for.

She hadn't thought to check for a ring, but she would at the next opportunity.

Riley glanced around the theater. The audience was mostly women she guessed to be in their forties or older. She and Zippy were a minority as twenty-somethings, although Riley begrudgingly asserted her thirties now since her thirtieth was next month. She guessed the men in Irish Thunder were close to her age.

"Excuse me, are you Riley?" A woman's Irish accent cut into her thoughts.

Riley looked up at a red-haired woman wearing a black headset. She wore heavy eye shadow and thick false lashes. Her long silk duster hung down the sides of a low-cut tank top, her bulbous cleavage front and center.

"Yes, I am." A smile spread across Riley's face.

The woman offered her a large, long-stemmed red rose. "This is for the second half of the show. When you hear a song about a rose, lift it high above your head."

Riley accepted the rose with a quizzical look. "Why are you giving it to *me?*" She peered at the name tag on the woman's tank top. "Siob—"

The woman tapped her nametag. "It's pronounced Sha-VAWN. I'm a roadie." She tilted her head to listen to her headset, then spoke into her mic. "Be right there." She turned to Riley. "Got to run. Enjoy the rest of the show." She hurried off and disappeared through a stage door.

Riley stared after her, puzzled. She closed her eyes and brought the flower to her nose, breathing in its soft fragrance.

Balancing a glass of red wine, Zippy scooted past and sunk into her seat. "I met some fun ladies from Alaska and California who invited us to party with them later." She stared at the rose, then at Riley. "Where'd you get the flower?"

Riley shrugged. "A woman gave it to me. She wore a headset, so she must be part of the crew. She said the flower was for the second half of the show. When I hear a song about a rose, I'm supposed to lift it up."

Zippy nodded dramatically. "I see what's happening here. Killian with a K had it delivered to you."

Riley shook her head. "You don't know that."

"Yeah, okay. I must have imagined him giving you 'the look' inside our stateroom and onstage just now. Open your eyes, Riley. See what's in front of you." Zippy bugged out hers for emphasis.

"He'd be like every other man in my life. Nice in the beginning, then would bail when he got to know plain, boring me." Riley was used to disappointment where men were concerned and refused to waste any more time getting her hopes up.

Zippy shot her a look of reproach. "Okay, Miss Pessimistic. How about a big fat kernel of hope for a change?" She downed the rest of her wine. "If you throw positive vibes out to the universe, they'll circle back to you. Trust me on that one."

Riley placed the rose on her lap, wondering how Zippy could be so positive about everything. The lights dimmed. A man who introduced himself as Rex stepped to a mic.

"Ladies and gents, *failte!* Now repeat after me, FOAL-cha."

The audience repeated. "FOAL-cha."

"Very good. It's Irish for 'welcome.' Welcome to the second half of our show. Now that you've moved around and imbibed in a beverage or five, this is the part of our show where we'll have fun. You can be as rowdy as you please."

The devoted fans in the audience knew exactly what was coming, and they whooped and hollered with anticipation.

"Here we go," sing-songed Zippy. "This is what we missed in Vegas."

"Remember," said the announcer, holding up his

forefinger. "What happens in the Caribbean stays in the Caribbean. Take it away, boys!" He backed away and scooted off the stage as the drums pounded a lively beat.

Irish Thunder hit the stage in full kilt regalia: short black jackets over white shirts, paired with forest green kilts, knee socks, and black tap shoes. The four men tap-danced onto the stage with fancy footwork and struck a pose.

A troupe of four women followed, then flanked the four men, with two on either side. A straight line of Irish dancers spread across the front of the stage, near the proscenium. They struck a starting pose with straight arms and crisscrossed legs.

The dance began with a rhythmic tapping of feet. Drums kicked in to punctuate the beats. Irish Thunder backed up and let the women take the stage for their high-spirited, dynamic performance. When it ended, the audience cheered.

A country western tune played, and Killian moved forward. A woman entered with long dark hair and a red strapless bodice over a floor-length black skirt with a slit to the top of her thigh.

Zippy leaned into Riley. "Check out Killian's kilt. Yeah, baby!"

Riley did more than check it out. She outright gaped, impressed with Killian's singing and dancing talent. The way he stood told her he deserved to be onstage—and then some.

The woman launched into a country western tune, her hands on Killian as he played the standoffish lover to her sexy siren song.

The country song ended, and the woman exited, while Killian stepped to the lip of the stage. In a clear, high tenor, he sang the opening lines a cappella—from a song Riley remembered her mom had played when she was younger: "Kiss from A Rose," by Seal, a popular British vocalist from the nineties.

Killian drifted down the stairs and moved up the side aisle with nonchalant grace. A bright, lavender spotlight roved around the audience, as if searching for someone.

Zippy elbowed Riley. "Do what the lady told you—get your rose in the air!" She hoisted Riley's arm, and Riley lowered it, heart pounding. The spotlight found her and stayed.

"Come on, get it up there!" Zippy grabbed Riley's arm and raised it higher this time.

Riley's breathing came fast as Killian moved toward her, his eyes trained on her. His movement was slow and hypnotic, as if in a dream. He arrived at her row and motioned her to where he stood in the side aisle, still singing. He didn't miss a beat.

Riley's heart thundered. *What if I have a heart attack? What if I faint?*

"Go, Rye! Go!" Zippy pushed her out of her seat with one foot on her butt. Riley scooted to the aisle, holding her rose, poised for fight or flight. Heart palpitating, she stood facing Killian as he sang, backed by the harmony of the singers onstage, watching him put the moves on a member of the audience.

The thing was, Riley loved this song. To have this devilishly handsome man singing it to her was surreal, and the thrill of his fabulous voice bubbled up inside her.

Her eyes dropped to his hand. *No ring.*

She shifted her eyes to his confident, self-assured ones. The intensity of his gaze raced her heart, and she couldn't look away.

Killian slowed the last two lines of the song about the blooming rose. When he finished, his hand lifted Riley's chin, and before she knew what was happening, his lips brushed hers in a gentle kiss. A shallow one—no tongue exchange—but who cared? A kiss was a kiss, and his lips tasted of peppermint.

The audience went bonkers, clapping, whistling, and squealing as he marathon-kissed her. Zippy jumped up and down behind her, clapping and laughing.

"Go Rye!"

Killian broke the kiss and slid his gaze downward. He plucked the rose from her hand, winked, and headed back onstage.

Riley failed miserably to throttle back the dizzying current electrocuting her system.

"Hey! Earth to Riley! Come sit down," Zippy stage whispered from her seat.

Imprisoned in a silken cocoon of euphoria, Riley swiveled her head at Zippy, who motioned her to take her seat. Riley's feet drifted along on a cloud as she floated to her seat in la-la land.

Zippy was beside herself and rapid-fired questions. "Is he a good kisser? What was it like? Did you slip him the tongue? Why did he take the rose back?"

Bewildered, Riley shook her head. "Don't know why he took my rose. Nor do I care."

And she didn't. The fireworks in her brain from Killian's kiss burst in slow motion each time she recalled him coming toward her and the feel of him once he was there. Bliss had a solid grip on her, and she barely registered the loud pulsating beat pounding the theater as Irish Thunder gyrated to a hip-hop song. Off came the jackets, and they twirled and tossed them. The audience jumped to their feet, screaming for more.

Riley had a tough time with the sudden transition to rowdiness—The Rose Kiss had gloried her to the point of ecstasy. Her freeze-frame of the exact moment remained as the Irish Thunder show continued; replaying it from inside her fog, until Killian snagged her focus, and she followed his every move.

The men peeled off their vests. The music had changed to a seductive melody as they unbuttoned their shirts.

One woman screamed, "Take it off! Take it *all* off!"

Irish Thunder played it up and undulated to the beat. The shirts came off and all that remained between the male dancers and the ladies in the audience was a layer of light woolen pleats. Four women danced out from the wings and scooped the clothes from the floor after the four men had discarded all but their kilts.

The guys bounced off the stage and danced through the audience. Killian stayed on the opposite side of the theater from Riley and Zippy.

"Come over here, Killian! Let's examine those pecs!" Zippy waved him over.

To Riley's disappointment, he stayed where he was. Two of the dancers lifted kilts, revealing their firm, manly buns, but kept their fronts covered, much to Zippy's dismay.

The performers moved in a classy way that was seductive yet avoided anything too scandalous. The two which Riley surmised from the playbill had to be Declan and Sean flexed and wiggled their pectorals. The men headed onstage to take their bows, leaving the audience on a high note.

Riley and Zippy stood with everyone else on their

feet, clapping and whistling, showing the performers they loved them. Irish Thunder waved, stepped back, and the curtain closed. No encore, much to Riley's disappointment.

Zippy could hardly contain herself. "Rye, Killian came all the way back here to give you a kiss! He remembered you, after holding your good-luck thong."

"Good luck thong? Cute, Zip." Riley found it impossible not to smile. "He was being nice, knowing how embarrassed I was earlier." Riley's emotions whirred like a blender on a frappe setting, but outwardly she fought for calm. "Don't worry. Guys like him don't go for boring, introverted geeks."

Zippy grimaced. "Don't say that about yourself. Plenty of people find you intriguing. This week, promise me you'll meet people. Get out of your comfort zone. Take risks."

Riley gave her an eye roll, wishing it were that easy.

Zippy grasped her shoulders. "Look at me."

Riley crossed her eyes and stuck out her tongue.

"Stop it, silly. Promise me you'll try. Do it for me, okay?" Zippy stared at her. "I saw the look on your face after Mister Kissy Face came back here and lip-locked you. I've never seen you like that. Open your eyes to possibility and stop judging."

Riley threw up her arms in resignation. "Okay, okay. Geez, no pressure or anything."

Zippy linked her elbow with hers. "Now let's go have fun."

Riley wished she had Zippy's confidence. Her dance card hadn't exactly overflowed in recent years. She didn't consider herself a special catch, so it was easy to remain safe and comfy in her alone world. There were no broken hearts there. No judging. No pretending to be someone interesting when she wasn't.

She didn't know why Killian had chosen her from hundreds of gorgeous women in the audience—but she was happy he had. His kiss would be something she'd forever remember.

Because that's all The Rose Kiss would ever be—a glorious memory.

Chapter 7

Killian

Killian awoke to a gentle rocking in the ship's bow as it encountered a light chop while sailing toward the Bahamas. The ship's motion didn't nauseate him as he'd expected. It was more of a gentle rock-a-bye to sleep kind of thing. Except it was time to get up.

He rolled over and stretched before easing himself from the comfortable bed. He hadn't expected a good night's sleep after getting hyped during last night's show. At least they got through it without anything going wrong. No busted guitar strings. Sean didn't fall on his arse during the anthem. Declan didn't cuss into his hot mic. Willy stayed on pitch.

And it had been Killian's turn to kiss an audience member. The four took turns and sang songs of their choice when alternating shows. Killian favored Seal's song because he sang it well and women loved it. He especially enjoyed Riley's reaction after sending Siobhan to give her the rose.

He'd taken it back and kept it as an excuse to see Riley later in order to return it. He thought of asking her to dinner. They'd be docking at Nassau, and he could take her some place nice.

Rex prohibited the Irish Thunder group from consorting with audience members while on the cruise, so Killian would have to be sneaky about it. The men viewed Rex's strict rules as completely ridiculous, but they abided by them to keep their jobs. Rex insisted on preserving their 'good boy' image. He even had strict guidelines for the stripping portion of the show. No vulgarity or crudeness to maintain a certain decorum.

Rex tapped on Killian's stateroom door and poked his head in. "Here's today's schedule. You have a meet and greet later this morning: take photos and sign autographs. This afternoon we'll take the launch onshore where we'll picnic with a few select fans. They paid extra for the platinum deal to have lunch with Irish Thunder on a section of beach."

"Is there any free time today?" Killian sat upright and ran his hand over his stubble.

"Not 'til after the show tonight," said Rex.

Killian reflected on the woman he'd kissed. He wanted time to know her better, but Irish Thunder's tight rehearsal and entertainment schedule would make that a challenge.

He took a quick shower and dressed. His stomach growled as he headed to the private VIP dining room, where the chef came out to take his order of a loaded omelet, extra crispy hash browns, and toast.

The meet and greet Rex had scheduled started soon, so Killian downed a coffee, then dressed for the onboard fan event. Rex specified white shirts and suit pants since it was in an air-conditioned room inside the ship.

Declan grinned as Killian sauntered in. "How's it hanging, Kils? Figured you scored last night after that epic kiss you planted on the American chick." He slapped Killian's shoulder. "Thought Rex would stomp out there and split ya's up."

Killian laughed. "She felt good. Why stop?" He said it for Declan's benefit, but it was true. She *had* felt good. "How long is this meet and greet thing, anyway?"

Willy made a sour face. "Too long."

The first of the fans entered the room and stood off to the side. Rex greeted them. "Good morning, ladies. Step this way to talk to the boys. They're glad to see you."

A plump older woman with crooked lipstick sidled up to Killian. "You're my favorite," she gushed. "I love watching you perform."

"Thank you. You're very kind." He reached for her hand and shook it.

During these meet-and-greets, Killian invariably squirmed when women of a certain age flirted with him. These superfans crushed on the Irish Thunder performers like groupies.

These ladies loved their music though, and Rex insisted on treating every fan as if they were the *only* fan. In the name of show business, Killian plastered on a smile and let the women hug him. Some wore strong perfume, watering his eyes. He reminded himself he enjoyed making others happy with his singing and his music, if only for a moment.

The problem was, he wasn't happy. Part of him loved performing, but the other part yearned to be free from all this, to do what he wanted when he wanted.

And to be with whomever he wanted. The restraints of this world he'd fallen into suffocated him.

He had decisions to make. And he'd better get going on making them.

Chapter 8

Riley

Riley argued with Zippy on the way to the meet and greet room, where her bestie had paid extra to shoot the breeze up close and personal with the men in Irish Thunder.

"You didn't tell me you paid for this bonus thing," Riley grumbled to her friend. "You know I hate being around lots of humans."

Zippy invoked her motherly tone. "I know I talked you into this cruise, but please humor me and come to this."

Riley noted a group of women staring at her and whispering. "They're gossiping about me because I kissed Killian last night," she said out the corner of her mouth.

"Correction. *He* kissed *you*." Zippy steered Riley into a room with a bank of windows on one side and a bar on the other. Irish Thunder stood behind a row of tables in front of the windows, greeting guests.

"Hey, mimosas!" squealed Zippy, hustling to the bar.

Riley followed and stood watching the bartender make Zippy's drink. "How can you drink alcohol this early in the morning?"

"It's expected. A Caribbean tradition. Thank you,

sir." Zippy winked at the bartender when he offered her the flute of orange juice and champagne. She nudged Riley. "Go talk to your boy, Mister Kissy Face, over there. He keeps glancing over here."

"He's not my boy," quipped Riley. The last thing she wanted was to be thought of as a groupie, like many of the people here. She observed a few gushing at the men and scooting next to them for selfies. Riley headed to the bar for a piece of pineapple to nosh, disregarding that the intended use of the pineapple was to garnish fancy drinks.

"Hello, Riley," murmured a deep voice behind her.

Heart flipping, she turned while biting into a pineapple wedge. Juice squirted a bullseye into one exquisite eyeball owned by Killian O'Sullivan—in all his badass, panty-melting maleness.

His eye squeezed closed. He rubbed it with his fist. "Good aim you got there, lass."

"Oh—oh, geez, I'm so sorry." She snatched a napkin from the bar and handed it to him, embarrassed with herself.

"Juicy pineapples." He wiped his juiced eye, now red from her inadvertent squirt.

"Definitely the pineapple's fault." She peered up at him. "You should rinse your eye."

"I can see fine with the other one." With one eye closed, he reached behind her for his own piece of fruit.

Her gaze followed his hand to that luscious mouth, acutely aware hers hung open; he was disgustingly hot when he chewed, despite his red eye. She clamped her mouth shut and resisted the urge to check for drool.

"How are you doing, aside from hostile pineapple?" she asked, chewing slower, studying him.

He laughed, blinking. "Grand. And yourself?" His welcoming, gold-flecked eyes held her rapt attention until he swallowed, then her gaze fastened to his throat like a radar lock on a heat-seeking missile.

"Very well. Very good. Good and well," she babbled. Why was she talking as if she were in a Victorian romance TV series?

"I was thinking—I wanted to ask you—all right, will you have dinner with me tonight?" He waited for her reaction.

Her eyes flicked up to his toffee-colored pools.

Did he mean it, or was he joking?

"Do you feel obligated because you—we kissed last night?" she stuttered, her cheeks heating. Had she heard that correctly? No one this amazing had ever asked her to dinner.

"Obligated?" He wrinkled his nose. "Why would I feel obligated?"

"I don't know. Because, because…" She trailed off at a loss.

"I wanted to ask after meeting you yesterday." He seemed sincere, but she was wary of his intent. She figured celebrities like him were mostly after one thing and she also figured most women were happy to provide it. Just not this woman.

"Um, sure." The unexpected invitation spread heat through her cheeks.

He leaned in. "Let's go early, as I have a show tonight. The Blue Lobster on the Lido deck opens at four-thirty. Meet you there?"

Riley's chest fluttered like sea birds twittered inside it. "Sure. Okay." She couldn't help but wonder if he had some other hidden agenda. Probably just sex. She'd been down that road before.

"See you later, then." He moved off to the gaggle of fans clustered around the other performers, who smiled and signed autographs.

Did that just freaking happen?

Riley couldn't wait to tell Zippy. She glanced around, amused to see her friend flirting with Sean. Riley strolled out to the deck and grasped the teak railing so she wouldn't levitate up to the next galaxy. Who knew spilling her delicates down a flight of stairs would wind up with a dinner invitation with a sizzling entertainer? And a hot guy stripper at that!

Life sure had its surprises.

Riley hadn't brought dressy clothes: mostly tank tops and shorts. And she didn't want to wear Zippy's navy-blue dress two nights in a row.

She raced to her stateroom and flung open the closet, pawing through hangers for one of Zippy's dresses. Most wouldn't fit her since Zippy was smaller on top. She remembered a clothing shop on the main deck when she and Zippy had explored the ship. Heart racing, she snatched her purse and scurried out the door.

A woman welcomed her as she breezed into the clothing shop on the main deck.

"Hello," Riley said breathlessly. "A man asked me to dinner, and I need a nice dress."

She shot Riley a knowing smile and waggled her finger. "Come with me."

As she followed the salesperson, Riley inspected the price tags and gulped.

So what if I plunge into debt? I'm having dinner with a hot male who likes me for some mysterious, incomprehensible reason. '

This was a tremendous step for her—opening her mind to possibility, no matter how remote the chance anything would come of it. It was well worth the risk...*right?*

What's the worst that could happen? She was on vacation, where dating rules didn't necessarily apply. She had the freedom to do whatever she wanted without being judged for it.

*Dinner with Killian O'Sullivan...*she thought dreamily. Now *there* was a reason to sink into debt. And if the only reason was that he wanted to have sex with her, so what?

At least she'd have bragging rights even if she never saw him again.

Chapter 9

Riley

Zippy appeared more excited than Riley at the prospect of her bestie's dinner date with 'Mister Kissy Face', as Zippy now warmly referred to him. "This dress is killer! Where did you find it?" She held it up to herself and turned from side to side in front of the full-length mirror.

"Down on the main deck in the Nautilus Boutique shop we passed yesterday. Do you think going strapless screams 'I'm easy?'" She glanced down at her modest cleavage. "Or does it scream 'I'm geeky, but I can rock elegance when I feel like it'?"

"I take it the salesperson talked you into this, didn't she?" Zippy stepped back for a thoughtful once over. "I'm glad she did. The aquamarine color with the white sequins and embroidery says who you are. I love it. It makes you look feminine and hugs your figure perfectly."

Riley appreciated her bestie's compliment. "It only spiked my credit card a few hundred."

"Worry about paying it off later," said Zippy. "This is no time to obsess about cost. It'll be worth it, especially if Mister Kissy Face tries to get you out of it later." Zippy tossed Riley a pair of white peep-toed stilettos. "Stick these on. One look at these babies and trust me—he *will* get you out of that dress."

Riley rolled her eyes. "It's dinner, not an orgy."

The possibility of having sex with Killian had indeed crossed her mind, and the thought tingled her. She dismissed it; highly unlikely anything would happen in that department. Not with Miss Boring Geek of the Year. If there was a pageant for it, Riley was sure she'd be crowned with a cardboard tiara to yawns and snores by judges and the audience.

Zippy raced around the stateroom, gathering makeup and hair fixings. "First, let's get your face on," she said, dumping her makeup arsenal on her bed.

Riley protested, but Zippy would have none of it. "Told you this cruise would be a game-changer for you." Zippy grabbed eyeliner and poised the brush. "Look down."

"I don't think I'll have a job to go back to, Zip. Michael threatened to fire me if I didn't show up the following Monday." Riley remained as motionless as she could.

"Look up." Zippy came at her with a tube of mascara. "Michael won't fire you. You're too good at what you do." She squeezed her tongue between her teeth as she focused.

"I did what you said. Went in and boldly told him I was taking a week off. I didn't ask. Well, I did, but—" she shook her head.

Zippy drew back, agitated. "Hold still. Stop obsessing!"

She grabbed a tissue and dabbed at a renegade glob of mascara between Riley's eyebrows. "Forget him while you're on this cruise. This is *your* time. Not to mention you met a hot someone." Zippy pawed through the pile and plucked out a lip color.

Riley tapped her friend's shoulder. "Hey, Zip."

"Uh-huh, what?" Zippy paused in her quest to reinvent Riley's unsuspecting lips.

"Thank you for talking me into this." Riley's voice tremored. "I couldn't ask for a better friend. Don't know what I'd do without you."

Zippy hugged her. "Someone's got to watch out for you. We're here to have fun. Speaking of which…" She tugged out the hair tie and bobby pins holding Riley's bun in place. "Get rid of this. Let your hair down."

"Hey!" Riley elbowed her. "I enjoy wearing my hair this way. No muss, no fuss."

"It's too damn functional." Zippy set to work curling Riley's hair. "Your objective, may I remind you, is to disarm Killian O'Sullivan. I'll transform you like they do in the romantic comedies with those montage beauty makeovers, and you can rock the shit out of this. I should work for beauty pageants doing hair and makeup. There. Check it out." Zippy sat back, satisfied.

Riley stared at her reflection and didn't recognize herself. Zippy had waved her magic wand, making Riley not only attractive, but downright pretty.

"Whoa, I shifted into a movie princess. Thanks, fairy godmother."

"Oh, stop," Zippy pretended protest. "I do decent work. Now get out of here. I made friends with some wild-assed mountain chicks from Alaska, and we're pub-crawling tonight. We plan to hit all eight lounges."

Zippy opened their tiny fridge and retrieved a miniature bottle of Moscato. "One is an Olympic cross-country skier with fantastic stamina. She outlasts all of us."

Riley hoped she'd have a different kind of stamina. One that involved not fainting from nervous anxiety or saying the wrong thing. Anxiety kicked in big time. Her breathing came up short in tiny, punctuated gasps.

Zippy flew into action and produced a medium-sized makeup shopping bag. She rushed to Riley.

"Exhale! Inhale!" she ordered, holding the sack over Riley's nose and mouth.

Riley slapped her hand away, bulging her eyes at Zippy.

"Breathe normal! Twelve repetitions—slow the heck down!" barked Zippy like a take-no-prisoners aerobics instructor. "For gosh sakes, will I have to chaperone you?"

Riley slowed her breathing and calmed herself. She willed her heartbeat to stop hip-hopping to its own tempo.

Zippy stood with her feet apart, arms akimbo, shaking her head. "Dress you up and you freak out. Buck up, Sullivan, get a flipping grip."

She acted like Riley's mission was to infiltrate the CIA.

Riley sat back and flicked her eyes at Zip. "If I hyperventilate at dinner, I'll wind up passing out in my spaghetti. Celebrities aren't trained in first aid. They have people who do that for them."

Zippy shot her a look that would glaciate Death Valley. "So, don't faint. Keep your shit together. Or you'll have to deal with me. *Capeesh?*"

Riley would rather face an execution squad.

Chapter 10

Riley

Taking a deep breath, Riley looked over the seafood menu to still the fluttering in her chest. The hostess had seated her at a corner table in the dimmest area of the restaurant. A wall candelabra shed the only light, along with fake flickering candles on the tables.

Her stomach ricocheted as she waited for her dinner date. Wait, this wasn't a date—simply a dinner with another person on the cruise.

Holy mackerel, am I in denial?

Only because Killian had a rose delivered to her, kissed her in front of God and the entire cruise ship, and asked her to dinner—didn't mean this was a date. Her mind flipped back and forth, and she cursed herself for overthinking it.

"Sorry I'm late." Killian appeared next to the table.

Riley glanced up from her menu and gulped. Resplendent in a dark suit, he was quite the package to take in up close. Just as he was last night when he kissed her in front of everybody.

He slid into the booth across from her. "You look stunning."

She made a pretense of glancing around to distract from the possibility that she might faint. *Inhale one two three, exhale one two three.*

"You're talking to me, right?"

"Who else would I be talking to?" His eyes roved her, gleaming in the candlelight.

"Thank you," she said awkwardly. Zippy must have worked exceptional magic. "Why did you put us in this dark corner?"

He folded his hands and rested them on the table. "It's not that I don't want to be seen with you. My manager frowns on us consorting with fans on the ship. He views it as breaking the fourth wall."

"The fourth wall, as in interacting with an audience? Isn't that only during a performance?" She shot him a quizzical look. "We're consorting?"

"Rex's words, not mine." Amusement flickered in his eyes as they met hers.

Riley leaned forward and stage-whispered. "So this is a clandestine dinner. Don't worry, I won't tell," she teased.

Her playful remark caused a grin to spread across his fine face.

"Thanks for accepting my dinner invitation." He picked up a menu as a server set wine glasses in front of them and darted away.

Riley inclined her head and lowered her voice. "She won't tell, will she?" Her head motioned in the server's direction.

Killian leaned toward her and whispered back. "Probably. I'll deal with it." He winked at her.

The server reappeared to take their orders. Riley chose the seafood combo special, and Killian ordered the same. "A woman after me own heart," he said with an Irish inflection.

All day Riley had wracked her brain for a

conversation starter. "You're a good kisser," she blurted, just as the server returned with a bottle of Riesling. Riley wondered if the young woman lingered, hoping to catch some juicy conversation.

The server's eyes flicked to Killian and Riley regretted uttering her kiss comment.

Riley's timing sucked, and her cheeks heated. "Whoops—not what I meant to say."

Killian stayed quiet until the server left. "So, I'm a good kisser?" He brushed his hair back, amused.

Riley rested her elbow on the table, chin in her hand. "Do you randomly kiss audience members at every show?"

"We take turns." He lifted the bottle of Riesling and poured them each a glass.

"So, every four shows you kiss someone in the audience. How many kisses does that total in a year? Aren't you worried you'll catch a virus?"

Killian laughed. "Not so far. Knock on wood." He tapped the wood table with his knuckles. "Come to think of it, I've not done the math. But yours was the most fun."

"I'll bet you say that to all your adoring fans." Riley listened carefully to what he said and *how* he said it. She remained guarded but determined to enjoy this experience and not read too much into it.

"No, I mean it." He lifted his wineglass. "Here's to a kiss from a rose. *Sláinte.*"

She raised her own and repeated. "*SLON-cha.*" Riley clinked his glass and sipped. "You sing the Seal song well. I mean, *really* well."

Killian gave her an appreciative nod. "Have you noticed we have the same last name?"

"Except yours has an O in front of it. Wasn't plain old Sullivan Irish enough? Your people had to slap an O in front of it for good measure?"

He laughed. "I'm from Cork. And em, yeh, they're stubborn about their Irish heritage. Where are your people from, if I may ask?"

"You may." She lifted her chin. "First off, I live in Seattle. But my dad's grandparents lived in Avoca, Wicklow. Ever hear of *Ballykissangel?* An old TV series from the seventies my mom used to watch. They filmed it in Avoca."

"I remember hearing about it. Long before my time."

"What are you, ten going on thirty-five?" Riley took another sip, relieved he was easier to be with than she expected. She loved his gentle camaraderie, his subtle wit.

"Not quite. Yanked out a gray hair today, though."

"Oh, you poor thing," she teased, peering at his sandy hair. "Look's fine to me. Along with your—what you have going on under there—" she motioned at his chest. "I mean, you know, your wonderful voice and all." She tripped on her words.

He smiled at her. "Thanks."

The food arrived, and they ate, interspersed with comments about the weather.

Her peripheral noted Killian watching her carefully twist fettucine around her fork. Her eyes caught his as she shoveled it into her mouth. She stilled, hoping she wasn't grossing him out with her lust for pasta. She dropped her gaze and slowed her chewing, suddenly self-conscious.

She'd been dying to ask him. "What's it like to be a

male stripper—I mean, exotic dancer?"

"Stripper. We don't refer to ourselves as exotic dancers." He waved his arms comically. "That conjures up snakes and silk and shaking coins on a belly. Stripping is like any other job."

"Oh yeah, right." She snorted. "I mean, isn't it weird taking your clothes off for women you don't know?"

"As opposed to women I know?" His eyes flickered while twisting a fork in his pasta. "I don't just do it for women."

Curious, Riley scrutinized him. "You strip for men too?"

"Sometimes." Killian filled his mouth with fettucine. He took his time chewing.

Riley waited, knowing he had to eat as well as talk, with his tight schedule. Patience wasn't her strong suit.

He swallowed, and grinned. "Women sometimes bring their boyfriends and husbands to our shows."

"Do they mind if you lap dance their wives or girlfriends?"

Killian smiled. "Not in Vegas, no. Most are entertained by seeing how their ladies react." He dropped his napkin on his plate, and a server swooped in to remove it.

Riley sat back in her chair. "It's different on the ship where most of us don't have our boyfriends or husbands with us."

Killian motioned at her left hand. "I don't see a ring on your finger. So, you left your boyfriend at home?"

"Yes—I mean no, I don't have a boyfriend, so I didn't leave him at home. That is to say, if I had one to leave at home. Currently, that is." She berated herself for over-explaining when all she should have said was, *no, I don't have a boyfriend.* She gave herself an eye roll.

Killian appeared amused. He glanced at his phone and set it back on the table. His expression changed to serious. "Let's cut to the chase."

Riley tensed, and she rested her fork on her plate. Her pasta twisted in her stomach. "What do you mean? As in sex?"

His brows jumped, and her comment seemed to stupefy him. "Why do women invariably jump to that conclusion?"

"Hmm, let's see." Riley gave him a crafty look. "Could it be because that's what you males habitually think about?"

"Ha, you have a point there. Actually, I meant something else." He captured her eyes with his. "I have to make the most of what little time I have."

Riley's hand flew to her heart. "Oh no, are you terminally ill?"

Killian gave her a surprised laugh. "No, it's—I never have time for the things I want to do."

"What is it you want to do?" she asked.

His eyes clung to hers. "Give me your hand."

She offered it, assuming he wanted to shake it.

He flipped her hand over, palm up.

"Are you a palm reader?"

Killian grinned. "Nah, that was my other life. Close your eyes." He placed something in her hand.

Opening her eyes, she studied the wilted, wine-colored rose and smiled.

"You were supposed to have this, but I kept it so I'd have an excuse to see you by returning it." His words floated into her ears like his unforgettable melody of last night.

She stared at the wilted flower, dumbfounded. "Are you toying with me? You don't need an excuse. You're a famous celebrity. You can have anyone you want."

He steadied his gaze on her. "Can you meet me tonight after the show?"

"I'd say that's cutting to the chase." She had trouble believing his sincerity. Had someone made a bet with him?

"I'll give you a hundred bucks if you date the geek."

"Where do you want to meet?" Excited shivers sprinted along her spine.

"There's a private VIP deck adjoining our suite on the ship's bow. I'll text the directions. Regular passengers aren't permitted in the VIP suites. I'll buzz you in and smuggle you up to the deck. It's a quiet place where we can talk."

She gave him a mischievous smile. "Smuggle me? Sounds covert. Should I dress as a ninja? Always fantasized about being one." She spread her fingers and swept them over her eyes.

Killian laughed. "Female ninjas are a turn-on for me, actually." He sat back, scrutinizing her. "You hide a lot of funny under that serious exterior."

"I'm not serious *all* the time." The wine gave her courage. "I do have other talents."

His brows shot up. "I'll bet you do. The most obvious is your dry sense of humor. And of course, your knockout looks. But I've a sneaking suspicion you don't realize that about yourself. When I saw you last night, I hardly recognized you, but tonight, you're even prettier. Not that you weren't when I first met you," he added quickly.

She felt compelled to explain. "Zippy piled this

makeup on me and fixed my hair..." she trailed off, embarrassed.

"That's not it. It's your—I don't know—disposition. You seemed stressed out the first day on the stairs. Last night I saw you happy and relaxed, like someone who embraces life. Tonight, I saw someone at peace with herself."

"Such astute observations." Riley managed a tentative smile. "You're talking about *me*, right?"

He tilted his head, studying her. "Vanity doesn't suit you. How refreshing. Not what I'm used to."

She had the urge to launch herself over the table to hug him. "That's the nicest thing anyone's said to me in a long while."

"People should say more nice things to you." He glanced at his phone. "I have to go. Are we on for tonight?"

"Do I need a password or a secret handshake? Eye, face, fingerprint recognition?"

He chuckled. "You read a lot of crime novels?"

"A fair share. Do you read books?"

"What do you take me for, a heathen? Of course, I read books, I'm Irish." He pretended to be offended. "You think I'm shallow-minded because I strip."

"No, no, that's not what I meant." Riley's cheeks heated while she scrambled to back pedal her insinuation. She hadn't meant to insult him. "I once read about an exotic dancer who has a PhD in mechanical engineering. She strips to blow off steam and says it's great exercise."

"Just so happens I have deep thoughts now and then." He gave her a smile that raced her pulse. "Really. You'll see." He offered her his hand.

"You're anything but shallow." Riley hated when she botched conversations. She accepted his hand, and he helped her to her feet.

He didn't let go. "Just giving you a hard time. See you at tonight's show?"

She glanced at her hand in his. "Will you be kissing me again?"

"You want me to?"

Riley pursed her lips and closed an eye as she considered. "I'm up for it if you are."

"Sorry, Irish Thunder doesn't play favorites," he teased.

"How about Sean? Send him over. Zippy has a thing for him."

"She does?" Killian let out a quiet whistle. "Sean's the wild one. Zippy would have her hands full. You don't want to know what *he* does with his hands—"

Riley cut in. "And on that note, you should go or you'll be late," she said brightly.

"Watch for my text, lass." He strolled off, then about-faced and returned, looking sheepish. "Hard to text without a phone number."

Riley commanded the leprechauns inside her chest to calm the heck down and cease and desist their jumping jacks. She recited her number in a blasé manner—like she did this routinely with hot entertainers on cruise ships.

"Break a leg or a kilt—or whatever." Her eyes flitted to his crotch, and she jerked herself upward to park her gaze on his face.

"See you after the show." He winked and sauntered off, catapulting Riley's heart up to orbit the moon and hurtle past Venus for good measure. She watched his delightful backside until he disappeared out the door, still mystified at his wanting to see her again.

I didn't bore him into next week?

If Killian's turn-on was a female ninja, hers was his sexy Irish accent. All he had to do was open his mouth. *Now, who was the shallow one?* Her feelings for this Irishman had nothing to do with reason, and she couldn't wait to peel back his layers…or his kilt, for that matter. Riley shocked herself with her racy thoughts.

I could get used to this taking-more-risks stuff.

It was time to unleash her libido as she closed in on her third decade.

Chapter 11

Killian

Killian breezed backstage after the Irish Thunder show, his chest and back shiny from sweat. He planned to shower in his suite, where he could catch his breath and relax before meeting Riley.

He texted her the directions to meet him on his way to the green room.

—Follow the main deck toward the bow, and you'll see a door with a lock pad. Text me when—

There was a tap on the dressing room door, and Mariah poked her head in.

Killian let out an exasperated sigh. "Privacy please. I'm changing."

"You used to love it when I walked in while you were naked." Mariah stepped into the room and moved up behind him as he stood in his kilt. She ran her palm over his sweaty back and he flinched.

"I haven't had a shower," he said irritably, attempting to finish his message to Riley.

She peeked around him to read his phone. "Who are you texting?"

"No one of consequence." He hit 'send' and pocketed his phone. He didn't finish it, but Riley would get the gist of it.

"Thought we could spend tonight together, like we

used to do. I've hardly seen you since we closed Vegas. Now we're busy with this new show." She moved to the front of him and rubbed her palms on his chest.

Killian brushed her hands away and stepped back. "No, Mariah. We ended this, remember? We're done."

Her dark eyes flashed with impatience. Mariah was a gorgeous woman, no doubt about it. Even with her fake boobs and face lift. Pushing into her forties, her age showed—a blight for a woman in the competitive entertainment business.

"We are *not* over. I agreed to back off and give you more space, like you'd asked. You're still taking me home to meet your family in Cork, right?" She gave him a demure smile. "You promised."

"Haven't promised you anything," said Killian. "I have to go. I'm knackered and need sleep." This woman was like a sticky bug trap, hard to pull away from.

"Come on, one drink. Like old times." She reached under his kilt. Her hand around his balls startled him, and he shoved her away.

"Stop it, Mariah! No more."

"You never used to want me to stop. It was always, 'more, Mariah, more, don't stop.'"

Killian cut in. "Things are different now. I'm different. What we did is in the past. Leave it there." He plucked his white shirt from a chair and grabbed the rest of his clothes. "How about we agree just to be friends? We work together, so let's just make this easy for both of us."

"Easier for *you*, you mean." She flipped her hair behind her. "I'm not a piece of trash you can cast aside. You and I loved each other. That counts for something."

"No, Mariah. I never said I loved you." He leveled

his gaze. "We only had sex, which I now realize was a bad decision. But let's be clear about this: I never told you I loved you." He despised himself for having had sex with Mariah. He'd screwed up big time.

Her eyes flashed. "You'll regret saying that."

Killian heaved out a sigh. "Don't make threats, Mariah. We need to keep things professional."

"It's time you knew something—"

He cut her off. "Sorry, gotta go. Have songs to work on." He forced a quick smile, then dashed out the door. He didn't have time for another one of Mariah's infamous rants.

Killian eyed the hanging moon as he hurried along the deck to the suite of VIP staterooms. He glanced at his phone to gauge the time. *Damn*, he was late to meet Riley. He tried texting and calling, but cell service was spotty on this fecking cruise ship, and he couldn't reach her.

He only had a week on this cruise with little time of his own to spend. He'd made up his mind to spend what time he could with Riley—and hoped she wanted to do the same.

Chapter 12

Riley

Riley checked her phone for the millionth time.

"Has Mister Kissy Face texted yet?" asked Zippy.

"Not yet." Riley didn't think Killian was the type to stand her up. He seemed sincere when he'd asked her to meet him after the show.

"Come with me to the Calypso Lounge on the pool deck. There's a band playing, and you can hang with me and the Alaska girls for a while," suggested Zippy.

"Sure, I'll come with you." Riley didn't come on this cruise to sit in her room.

Zippy elbowed her friend. "You said he paid you wonderful compliments, like how pretty you are."

"Yeah, he did."

"Don't worry, you'll see him. He's bound to be someplace. He probably had show stuff to take care of. Performers are busy people."

"I suppose," said Riley, hoping her friend was right. She pressed the elevator button, and when it opened, they stepped in.

Zippy pressed the button for the main deck. "Hasn't it crossed your starstruck mind he may have invited you to his private deck to have his way with you?"

"His *way* with me? Who are you, Emily Brontë?" Riley figured it had only been a matter of time before

Zippy got around to the sex quotient.

So what if he'd invited her for an erotic play date? It would be the most excitement she'd had in a long while. What's not to like about sex on a cruise with the ship's smoking hot entertainment? The thought of it tingled her, and she found herself hopeful for the opportunity.

The women made their way to the pulsing beats emanating through the walls and windows of the Calypso Lounge. Bodies crammed the dance floor, swaying to the Caribbean beat.

"Zippy!" a woman called out. She waved the two friends over to sit with her.

Riley followed Zippy to the table, and people scooted to make room for them to sit. "I'll get us drinks!" shouted Zippy over the loud music, heading to the bar.

A tap on Riley's shoulder caused her to look up. It was Sean, from Irish Thunder. He bent to speak in Riley's ear. "Want to dance?"

Why not? She hadn't heard from Killian. She rose and followed Sean to the dance floor in his Hawaiian shirt, shorts, and flip-flops. Riley had changed from her dinner dress to shorts and a tank top. The balmy Bahama weather and warm air pleasantly required it.

They danced a fast song. When it ended, Riley asked Sean, "Do you know where Killian is?"

He shook his head. "He's usually with Mariah after the show."

Riley played it cool while her heart cracked in half. "Mariah?"

"You know, the female vocalist in our show. They've been off and on for a while now," Sean said matter-of-factly.

Zippy appeared next to Riley and offered a look of concern. She handed Riley a glass of wine. "I'm thinking you need this."

Riley took the wine and wandered to the table and plopped down on a chair, checking her phone. *Still no text.*

Sean and Zippy joined her, and Riley pointed to her phone, hollering over the pulsating music. "Zip, text me. See if we have cell service right now. I only have one bar."

Zippy nodded and worked her thumbs while Riley waited. Nothing came through.

"No service!" yelled Zippy, shrugging.

Riley stood and wandered to the deck outside. She debated walking up to the VIP deck and knocking on the door. But she didn't want to get Killian in trouble with his manager for 'consorting.'

Zippy followed her out. "There's an after-hours party near the Indigo Lounge. Want to check it out?"

"Nah, I'll just go to our room. I'm tired and need some downtime."

"Are you sure?" Zippy put a hand on her shoulder. "I'm sorry, Rye. Want me to send Sean to go look for Killian?"

"No, no. The last thing I want is to seem needy." Riley forced a smile. "Go have fun."

"Okay. See you later." Zippy disappeared into the lounge.

Riley ambled to the stateroom and got ready for bed. Water pooled in her eyes, and she stubbornly forced it back. No way would she shed tears over someone she hardly had anything going on with, except a dinner, a kiss, and a wilted rose.

She stared at the spent flower on her nightstand, contemplating whether to slide the door open and heave it into the sea. Add Killian to the lengthy list of men who'd lost interest, she thought glumly.

Riley undressed and slipped on her baby-doll nightie. Moon wash glistened the water as the ship rested dockside in Nassau. It was too beautiful to stay inside. She took a pillow and blanket outside to the lounger on the balcony. The warm ocean breeze and water gently lapping lulled her to sleep.

"Riley." A man's voice called her name. "Riley, wake up."

Her eyelids fluttered, and she opened them to see Killian seated in the chair next to her. She jerked herself upright, instantly awake, gawking at him.

"Killian! What are you doing here?" She did a double take, peering through the glass door into the stateroom. "How did you get in? Where's Zippy?"

"Ran into Zippy and Sean at the Indigo Lounge. She gave me her key card, said you'd be here. I knocked, but no answer. Zippy said to let myself in, that you're a heavy sleeper."

"Gee, thanks Zippy, that's not weird or anything," she muttered. She turned to Killian with a frenzied look. "I might have been in the shower."

He shot her an impish grin. "Yeah, that would have really sucked for me. I'm not a serial killer, remember?"

She narrowed her eyes. "Uh-huh. How do I know you aren't a perv?"

His impish grin widened. "I can be on occasion. You didn't get my messages?"

"No. Cell service sucks on this ship."

"Yeah, I gathered." He glanced at the shimmering

waves, then back at her, the harbor lights reflected in his eyes.

Riley tugged her coverlet up to her neck, aware of her low-cut nightie. "Where did you go after the show?"

"Back to my room and showered, then texted you. I waited for you to text me back."

"You should have told me ahead of time where to meet you." She didn't want to make him feel bad about it; she didn't know what he had going on. "You can't depend on this shitty cell service." She motioned at her stateroom. "That's why we have room phones."

"Forgot about that. So used to relying on my mobile. Or cell, as you Americans call it." He gazed at the tranquil ocean, glimmering in the moonlight. "I apologize things got screwed up. Let's start over."

Riley laughed. "We're long past introductions. Since you wanted to cut to the chase, now it's my turn." She said it in a teasing manner, which seemed to put him at ease.

A flash of humor crossed his face. "Fire away."

"Are you with Mariah—that woman in your show— like in a relationship?"

Killian pulled back in surprise. "Why would you ask that?"

Riley shrugged. "Sean said you might be with Mariah tonight, when I couldn't find you. He said you and she have been together for a while, so I figured you still were."

Killian shook his head vigorously. "Not anymore. It's over now."

"So you weren't with Mariah tonight?" Riley studied him closely, ready for the worst. "I know it's none of my business—"

Killian cut in. "No, I wasn't with her. Well, I was, but just talking—look I don't know why Sean would say we were together." He stared out at the shimmering waves. "You need to know something. I'm not that guy who plays women. Never have, never will. Rex hired Mariah a few years ago. We were involved for a while, and I ended it."

He scooted his chair closer and closed his hand over hers.

"I want to be with *you* tonight. Do you believe me?" Gold glinted his dark eyes, and his tender expression caused her breath to rush out.

"I want to. You seemed so sincere at dinner." Her heart knocked around in her chest.

"I was. I am." He stood and moved to her lounger, lowering himself next to her. "I want to show you how sincere I am."

She couldn't deny herself if he wanted to touch her, but she wanted to make the first move.

"I'd rather show *you* how sincere *I* am," breathed Riley. An unseen force propelled Riley's mouth toward his for a gentle kiss. Her heart levitated while he filled her senses. She fingered his hair, relishing the heat radiating from under his silk Hawaiian shirt.

He slipped his tongue into her mouth, gently massaging hers. She tasted peppermint. No man had ever kissed her this way, nipping her bottom lip and giving her soft kisses on the sides of her mouth.

"I believe your sincerity," he breathed, his lips moving along her skin.

Sparks exploded with electric intensity when his lips seared a path down her neck and shoulders. Wanting more, she tugged the coverlet away from her chest.

Killian had her under his spell, and she surprised herself by placing his hand on her breast.

When he hesitated, she scolded herself for her audacity.

"Sorry—I just—"

"It's all right. Don't want to go too fast." His arms came around and engulfed her. She pressed against him, and they stayed that way for a long while.

No words—just an embrace. He made no move to do anything except hold her.

"Kiss me again," she whispered. "You're unfailingly good at it."

He chuckled. "Unfailingly? No one's ever described me that way."

"It's time someone did," she intoned, wanting him to do anything he wanted.

He kissed her softly, as if she were delicate. She lost herself in him and brought her hands up, fisting them in his hair.

"Riley, I want to know you," he said in a husky voice. "And I want you to know me, aside from what I do in my entertainment world. If anything goes beyond that, well, I want it to be special."

"Define 'anything'." She looked into his moony eyes, and they smiled back at her.

"You know. Anything...like if we were to get along."

"We're getting along okay so far." She liked that he'd put on the brakes, so she wouldn't have to. Things were already moving at a brisk pace. She hadn't had time to catch her breath, much less figure out whether she liked Killian because of his celebrity, or was she attracted to him aside from that?

Killian peered into her eyes, melting her. "Tomorrow afternoon and evening we spend at sea. I have a picnic function in the morning before we leave the port. And rehearsal in the afternoon for tomorrow night's show."

"Sounds like your manager keeps you busy."

"Rex does that, all right. But I have an idea. The day after tomorrow, we'll be at the next port, in Costa Maya, Mexico. How about the two of us go ashore and make a day of it? Irish Thunder has the day and evening off."

The idea soared her spirits, launching her heart over the sea. Her newfound courage emboldened her. "Come closer for my answer."

He pressed against her, and she slipped her tongue into his mouth, controlling the kiss. His response was immediate. When she ended the kiss, she noted he was aroused. It elated her to have this effect on him.

His lids became hooded. "I take it that's a yes."

"At some point, will you please sing me the Seal song about the rose? With only me as the audience. Promise?"

"*Geallaim duit*. I promise." He touched her cheek.

Riley blinked, incredulous. She couldn't believe this wonderful person wanted to spend time with her. Her very soul rocketed over the starry constellations.

He stood to go. "Have to get ready for tomorrow."

Riley didn't want him to leave and found herself motioning him toward the bed.

"Want to lie with me for a while? You can stay on top of the covers. We can talk."

"I don't have self-control in that department." He lifted the sheet and comforter and motioned her under the covers. "Come here and I'll tuck you in."

"No one's tucked me in since I was five. You won't change your mind?" She patted the bed next to her.

He gave her a close-mouthed smile and lifted the covers over her.

"Sweet dreams, Miss Sullivan."

"Now I'll be dreaming about Irish guys in kilts." She wished he'd stay; so the magic wouldn't stop. She wanted this night to last forever. Morning would ruin it.

He blew her a kiss. "Count your sheep."

"Good night, Killian with a 'K'.

He moved to the door and paused.

"I see good things on the horizon. Sweet dreams." He let himself out and the door latch clicked.

"Well, how about them coconuts?" she said to the empty room, her mind still reeling. "I had a hot cutie in my room. Twice!" Unable to contain herself, she kicked her legs up and down and squealed.

Zippy's words about taking risks echoed.

Riley had opened possibilities with someone who was hot as the Bahamas sunshine. Dazed, she rolled over. But instead of counting sheep, she counted brawny-chested kilted Irishmen jumping over her bed.

And they all looked like Killian.

Chapter 13

Killian

Killian's phone alarm sounded at six a.m. He had to be on the boat shuttle by seven. Rex had arranged a superfans breakfast with Irish Thunder onshore near Nassau Beach before the ship left port.

This was the other reason he hadn't stayed with Riley last night. But mainly he preferred to be a gentleman and not sleep with her—though he'd wanted to.

Big time.

He'd had a stiffy so hard last night, he could have ram-rodded his way into a medieval castle.

After a brisk shower, Killian put on his terrycloth robe and shuffled out to the dining room in the VIP area the Irish Thunder cast and crew shared.

"You're sure chipper today," Sean commented as he tapped away on a laptop. "Wi-Fi isn't working. Can't get diddly with my phone."

Killian chuckled. "We must be in the Bermuda Triangle."

Declan looked up. "Hey, weird shit happens in the triangle. Seven-forty-sevens and huge freighters have disappeared without a trace. Don't you remember that sci-fi movie where all those things suddenly showed up on a desert?

Killian chuckled and poured the cream into his coffee. "Only a movie, Dec. It's not real."

"Oh, yes, it is!" Willy chimed in, noshing a cinnamon roll.

"You'll ruin your six-pack," said Rex as he breezed in and took his spot at the head of the table. He pointed at Willy's offending roll and guilted him into abandoning it. "You'll all have a healthy breakfast of fruit and protein waiting onshore."

Rex shifted his intimidating stare to Killian. "You stayed out late last night."

"Couldn't sleep." Killian swallowed his irritation and poured himself a coffee. "Took in some fresh air out on deck." It was partly true. Only the deck he had occupied was a wee bit smaller and he'd had a hard-on the size of Texas.

Rex drilled him with a stern stare. "From now on, stay on the VIP deck after our shows. No mingling with fans." He glanced at his wristwatch. "All right, lads, better get ready. We're due at the boat launch in fifteen. Don't be late."

He stood with his clipboard in hand, squinting at it through his cheaters. "Killian, your electric guitar will be pre-set for your duet with Mariah. The crew rigged the power cables since you'll be performing outside."

Killian wolfed his coffee and prepared to go ashore. The men wore their blue Irish Thunder tee shirts and tan board shorts. Sean and Killian put on their matching indigo baseball caps.

The cobalt seas had a light chop as the boats docked next to the ship. Killian and the rest of Irish Thunder stepped down the ladder onto the platform to board the launch. Good thing he wasn't hungover, or the choppy boat ride surely would have made him queasy.

Once on shore, Wanderlust Travel had arranged picnic tables and chairs in the sand, with a large volleyball area and net nearby, and a three-person calypso steel band playing upbeat songs on a wood platform.

Killian and Sean moseyed over to a small building surrounded by palm trees, where the smell of tasty food lured them. Irish Thunder and their crew dined first, so they could interact with their fans until it was time to perform.

Killian loaded his plate with fruit, scrambled eggs and sausage and headed to their private table, where the men could eat in peace.

"Hi Killian!"

A group of older ladies waved, pointing their phones at him. He plastered on his Irish Thunder smile and waved back. "How long does this thing last?" he asked as Declan and Willy sank onto the picnic bench across the table.

"Couple hours," said Declan between sips of coffee. "The ship leaves this aft for the next port."

Sean squinted. "Which port is next?"

"Costa Maya in Mexico," said Killian, and stabbed a sausage with his fork. "On the east coast of the Yucatán Peninsula."

"Well, aren't you a geographic marvel?" Sean elbowed him and his face changed. "Rut-roh. Here comes lover girl. Your turn to entertain her. I'm out of here."

Mariah headed for their table with food piled high on her plate as Sean made a fast getaway.

"Lovely," groaned Killian, watching her move

toward him with enough food to feed a platoon of sharks.

"Have fun, Kils." Willy raised his brows and rose to follow Sean.

Killian pointed his fork at Declan. "You leave me and you're a dead man."

"Guess you'll have to kill me, sport." Declan winked and escaped before Mariah swooped in.

The rats had abandoned ship before the kraken wrapped her tentacles around their table.

"Top of the morning, hot stuff. And how are we today?" Mariah shot Killian her winning smile.

The woman had incredibly white teeth despite the mass quantities of red wine and black coffee she consumed.

"Just grand," he gritted out.

"Ready for our duet? We should do a run-through to warm up."

"Nah, I'm good," he said, focused on the calypso band.

"I looked for you last night," she purred.

"Did you now?" he said, nodding and smiling at a fan who waved and took his photo.

Mariah waved her fork around. "None of those women want to take *my* photo." She stabbed a helpless piece of fruit and noshed it.

He bit his tongue to avoid saying, *maybe if you were a nicer person.*

Instead, he opted for, "Why don't you check out an all-male cruise?" He wished she'd take him up on it.

"And what would that be?" she said in an icy tone.

One of her finer attributes, he thought sarcastically.

"A sports´ cruise." Killian laughed. He thought it funny, even if she didn't think so.

He watched her shovel the food in, noting she'd gained a few pounds.

"Saw you heading to the Oceania Deck last night. All the way up on the 6th deck. I said to myself, 'Gee, I wonder who Killian knows up there.'"

"You had nothing better to do than monitor my whereabouts?" He tamped back his irritation at Rex and Mariah knowing every move he made; he must keep things professional out here among the fans who were his bread and butter.

"Imagine my surprise when you took out a key card, opened the door, and disappeared into Room 1532." Mariah displayed a fake look of wonder. "You were there quite a while, I might add."

"You not only followed me, but waited around to see when I'd leave?" Killian folded his hands and squeezed them together to control his anger.

Mariah gave him a demure look. "You know how Rex told us to watch out for each other."

"There's a difference between watching out and spying on each other."

So that's how Rex knew he was out late. Killian leaned forward, leveling his gaze. "It's in your best interest not to tell Rex where I go or what I do on this cruise." He rose and shot her a disgusted look. "And FYI…what I do is no longer your business."

He gathered his plate and coffee and ducked into a circle of fans. "Good morning, ladies!" he boomed out in his thick Irish accent.

"Anyone for a volleyball game?" Squeals of delight as Willy, Declan, and Sean joined him, and they organized two overly enthusiastic teams.

After a few games, Siobhan gave the signal it was

time for them to sing. She asked the crowd to take a seat on the grass or wherever they were comfortable.

The singers took their positions in the performance area. Declan called out to the steel band. "Give us a C major."

The woman on a steel drum clinked a tinkly note. The singers hummed the pitch and launched into a perfectly harmonized medley of Irish tunes.

When they finished, Declan stepped forward. After cracking a few jokes to get the crowd of about one hundred fifty laughing, he said, "And now, Miss Mariah and our boy Killian will sing a love song for you."

Siobhan handed Killian his electric guitar, and he plucked the intro to *Whenever You Come Around*, by Vince Gill. Mariah led off with her golden soprano, and Killian joined in with the harmony. It was a slow rhythm, a love song Killian used to enjoy singing with her.

Not anymore.

When things had gone south between them, Killian begged Rex to change this song. But Rex had refused, saying it was one of the most popular in their shows. Especially with Killian's killer solo on the electric guitar. Now, it rankled him to play-act a couple in love to make the song emotional and convincing.

When they finished to enthusiastic applause, phones pointed at them. Killian knew these photos would wind up on social media and in gossip columns.

He hoped Riley wouldn't see Mariah groping him like her personal man-toy.

"You sang perfectly. As always." Mariah took his hand. "Spend the day with me."

Killian pulled his hand away and lifted his guitar strap from his shoulder. "I have other plans."

He gave her a fake smile and strolled over to waiting fans who wanted selfies.

"You mean with Riley Sullivan?" she spat the name out after him.

Damn her.

Killian froze in his tracks, then spun around and strode toward Mariah, who stood smirking at him. "Let her alone. I don't want you near her, understand? She's nothing to you. I told you to move on with your life as I have."

He walked away, shaking his head, sick to death of others having a say about his private life. *Hell, what private life?*

It didn't exist. Everything he did was for this show to succeed. So many depended on him: cast, crew, everyone. People who worked on the Irish Thunder production fed their families and paid their bills because of himself, Sean, Declan, and Willy Boy.

He longed to write his own songs; play and sing them the way he wanted. A certain brown-haired American female drifted into his mind. She hadn't fallen all over him like most women. She didn't judge—she was genuine and unassuming, without pretense. And not infatuated with herself like so many in his world.

At least the entertainment business hadn't tainted Riley the way it had for women who'd sucked up to him, hoping to get money or a career boost.

His heartbeat kicked up a notch at the idea of seeing her later. It up ticked even more at getting off this effing cruise ship with her tomorrow, away from prying eyes.

That excited him more than anything.

Chapter 14

Riley

Zippy linked elbows with Riley, strolling along an outside deck on their way to an Irish dance class.

"You can't wipe that grin off your face."

Riley's grin widened. She enjoyed the ocean breeze teasing her spiraled curls. After her titillating evening with Killian, she'd risen early to apply makeup and curl her hair. She had a reason to look her best now.

"Killian came looking for you last night at the Indigo Lounge. He couldn't get hold of you after the show. I handed him my key card and said he'd have to wake you. It surprised me when he came back shortly after to return my card." Zippy jabbed her with her elbow. "He woke you and...did other things?" She wiggled her brows suggestively.

Riley's mouth curved up. "Yes."

"Yes, he woke you, or yes, he did other things?" Zippy's tone was urgent.

"We talked." Riley had experienced rapid intensity with Killian, and she was still processing it. Rather than talk about it, she wanted to bask in her internal bliss and let the unicorns dance inside her. She smiled down at the deck.

Zippy persisted. "Did he kiss you?"

Riley lifted her chin. "I kissed *him*."

"*You* took the initiative?" Zippy's jaw hung open.

"Who says men have to be the ones to make the first move? For once, I wanted to initiate things. You're the one telling me to take risks and be adventurous."

"I'm proud of you. Good job." Zippy pulled her in for a side hug. "At least *some* kissing got done. Doesn't matter who starts it. I'm happy for you, Rye. It's about flipping time."

Riley elbowed her friend. "Did any kissing happen on your end?"

Zippy swung her blonde hair behind her shoulder. "You know me. I'm in it for the conquest. We partied 'til dawn with the wild-assed, insane Alaskans." She steered them to a doorway of a large room where people had gathered.

"This is your Irish dance class?" Riley peered inside.

"You're doing this class with me." Zippy snatched her hand and led her into the room.

"I'm no dancer." Riley did an about-face for a fast exit.

Zippy clamped a hand on her wrist. "Oh no, you don't. You're staying here."

"If I stay, what do I get out of the deal?"

Zippy pursed her lips. "Killian will see you dance during the last Irish Thunder show."

Riley perked up. "Oh yeah? What if I can't do it?"

"You'll do it." Zippy made a V with two fingers and pointed at her own eyes, then at Riley's. "Just focus."

A woman with a long red braid addressed the class. "*Failte* everyone! Welcome to the Irish dance class. My name is Saorise—pronounced 'SUR-shuh'—I'm your instructor for the week. A little about me. I danced in a famous Irish dance show. You probably saw us on public television."

Riley observed Saoirse's posture to be the straightest she'd ever seen. A dancer's body, for sure. Riley automatically straightened her own spine and pulled in her abdomen.

"I'm a slouch next to this woman," mumbled Zippy, mimicking the instructor's posture and lifting her chin.

Saoirse instructed. "Let's begin. Spread out and give yourselves space. The steps are simple. We'll learn the dance in wee bits. Assume this start pose and we'll begin with a one-two-three step. First, I'll demonstrate. We'll take it nice and slow." Saoirse stood tall with legs crossed. "I have our dancers scattered around the room to help. Watch them if you have difficulty. Ready? Here we go."

"Yeah right, she makes it seem easy," groused Zippy, attempting the moves.

Riley frowned, shaking her head. "Not for me. Never took a dance class in my life."

Saoirse continued. "Start with right foot in front of our left foot, then hop, one, two, three. Then tap: One two, and one two and one two and kick…and one two and one two and one two and kick. Switch your feet and point, point, point, and back. Got it?"

A titter spread through the room as everyone tried to follow her sequence.

"No worries, folks. We'll repeat this until you'll be doing it in your sleep. Ready? Here we go." Saoirse counted through the sequence as she patiently demonstrated.

Riley and Zippy did their best to keep up. Toward the end of class, Riley had the hang of it.

"Hey, Zip, look!" She cycled through the dance

sequence and wonder of wonders if she didn't nail it.

"You're a freaking natural!" exclaimed Zippy, slack jawed. "You Irish have dancing in your DNA. Not like us Sicilians."

"Ladies! The hour is up, but you're welcome to stay and practice. You'll perform your Irish dance routine onstage for your fellow passengers during our last Irish Thunder performance in five days. See you tomorrow morning. Good job today." Saoirse and her instructors waved goodbye as the class filed out onto the decks.

Riley hopped up and down, bursting with excitement. "Zip, I'm not telling Killian we're doing this class. When he sees us dance on the last show, it'll blow his mind, don't you think?" Invigorating energy tingled every nerve in her body.

Zippy pulled back and observed her with a pleased expression. "I've not seen you this happy or excited since—forever. You go girl!" Her mouth twitched.

Riley rested her hands on the teak deck railing. "Look at that ocean, Zip! It's a sapphire blue. It's beautiful." Riley watched the gently rolling waters frosted with lazy whitecaps. "The ocean never stops moving, does it? Did you know Killian gets seasick? He said at dinner yesterday…" she trailed off, catching Zippy's wondrous expression.

"What?" Riley stared at her bestie.

"I wish you could see yourself. You're like a teenager after a first date. I love this. And if you stick those gorgeous locks into a bun again, I'll shave your head. Wear your hair down, it makes all the difference." Zippy studied her in a way Riley hadn't seen before—as if her best friend was seeing her for the first time.

Riley didn't know what made her

happier…Killian's attraction or Zippy's thrill at seeing her full of life and vigor and whatever else filled her heart at this moment.

The two friends strolled along the main deck. They paused in front of a giant screen displaying a slide show.

"Look, they're showing photos of the cruise." Riley stepped closer.

Killian's face popped up in mid-song, his mouth open.

A quiver sprinted through Riley, knowing that luscious tongue had been in her mouth—and she'd loved every delicious inch. His photo faded out and others faded in. Irish Thunder was onshore at a picnic, playing volleyball. Eating and talking with fans. Posing for photos. Irish Thunder singing. Killian and Mariah facing each other singing, with Killian playing his guitar. Mariah with her hands on Killian.

Riley's green monster reared its ugly head at the woman hanging all over Killian.

Zippy caught her scowl. "Rye, don't let it bother you. It's part of their act. You said he isn't with her anymore, right?"

"He said he ended it with her, but she acts like they're still together."

"It's not your deal, Rye. Don't worry about it. He's obviously into you, not her. Come on, let's change and go to the pool on the main deck, since we'll be at sea the entire day."

Riley brightened. "Great idea. I want to go down the water slide that spirals from the top of the ship to the swimming pool. If I can get the nerve."

"A couple of Long Island iced teas, and you'll be screaming down that puppy backwards with your eyes closed." Zippy made a dismissive hand gesture.

After they changed in their stateroom, the two besties gathered towels, sunblock, and their sunglasses and headed to the bow of the ship, where pools were full of swimmers and others occupied loungers on the deck. The three-person calypso band played on a platform next to the bar.

"I love calypso. Such cheerful music." Riley happily sipped on her straw, relishing the rum sliding down her throat. She and Zippy claimed their spot in the ship's bow, leaning against the pool's edge, soaking in the rays. Water swirled around their waists as they sat in the two-foot-deep pool, sipping umbrella drinks.

Riley watched spinner dolphins flirt with the ship's bow as it separated the waves on the way to the Yucatán Peninsula. The day was perfect. The sky and the ocean competed for all shades of cerulean brilliance that no artist could emulate.

And Killian…she wondered what he was doing right now. He said they had to rehearse for tonight's show, and he'd see her afterwards. This time he explained how to get to their suite, and he would meet her out front. He told her to come directly after the show and he'd be there.

She was at a crossroads. For once, she wouldn't plan every second of her day, or worry about what might happen. She'd cast her fate to the ocean breeze, go with the flow, and see where it blew her. She liked the direction it was blowing her now.

Riley stood on a precipitous cliff, poised to dive in. *Once I do…there's no going back.*

Chapter 15

Killian

Killian stood in the wings, ready to take the stage after Declan finished his solo. Tonight's Irish Thunder performance had a different format. Each man sang individually, highlighting their own style. Killian was the one with the most rock and roll vibe, and it drove audiences wild. Rex always saved him for last during the first half of the show.

"I did what you asked and moved Riley Sullivan and her friend to the front row VIP seats," said Siobhan, adjusting her headset. She pulled the stage curtain back and pointed.

"See? There they are." Siobhan poked him. "You owe me, hot boy."

Killian laughed. "Don't I always? You're a good friend." Siobhan had become like a sister to him after declaring that Killian had "it," meaning he had that unique stage presence that everyone in show business strove to emulate. She tagged him as the most talented Irish Thunder performer on all their social media sites.

"I knew the minute you gave Riley the rose something was up. Never saw you act that way with an audience member. The duration of that kiss spanned geologic time. Thought Rex would have a conniption." She smirked. "You like Riley, don't you? Good luck when Mariah finds out."

"Mariah already knows," said Killian. "She'll simply have to deal with it. We're done and everybody knows it. Everybody but her, anyway."

Declan finished his set, and the applause was Killian's cue to return onstage. Siobhan stood at her light board in the wings, hand raised, ready to signal Killian to enter.

Rex announced over the sound system. "And now I give you the fabulous recording artist and founder of Irish Thunder…Killian O'Sullivan!"

The house erupted with whoops and applause. When the applause diminished, Siobhan pointed at him.

"Go!" she stage-whispered, flipping switches on her light board.

The stage changed to an icy blue, displaying Killian's white shirt with his sleeves rolled partway up his forearms. His white pants fluoresced when he strolled out with his acoustic twelve-string.

A loud intake of breath met his appearance onstage. His head swiveled to the source, and he was pleased to find it was Riley. The look on her face was priceless. He preferred to consider it a look of lust.

Does she think I'm sexy? Grand…I can deliver sexy.

He lowered himself onto the tall stool and positioned the standing mic. In his sensual, come-do-me voice, he drawled, "Are we having a good time?"

His peppery gaze shot to Riley, who gave him a closed-mouth smile as whoops and hollers in the house responded enthusiastically. "I can't hear you, ladies. I said…" He moaned an exhale into the mic as if having sex with it. "Are we having a *good* time?"

The audience clamored with hoots and hollers. "We

love you, Killian!"

He milked it, loving the build of anticipation before delivering what they wanted.

A woman's voice hollered, "Take your shirt off!"

A large white thong landed on the stage in front of him. Laughter followed as he bent to retrieve it and held it high. "Someone lost this. Will the owner please come forward to claim it?"

Two older women trotted down the aisle, racing each other to the stage.

Killian tossed the thong to them, and they engaged in a tug-of-war, ripping the bloody thing in half. Killian bugged his eyes out and made an oh with his mouth and the audience ate it up, laughing and applauding. The ladies each held up their half and returned to their seats, triumphant.

He brushed back the sides of his hair and strummed, 'Brown-Eyed Girl.' He aimed a friendly wink at Zippy with her big brown eyes. She pretended to be embarrassed, but he knew she loved it.

When he ended, he immediately launched into 'All Out of Love.' The ladies loved this one. Rex reserved the love songs for Killian; not only did he sing them with emotion, he'd perfected a sexy yodel on the high notes.

Audiences loved it.

The band and the rest of Irish Thunder joined in upstage. "Here's a tune by Crosby, Stills, and Nash."

Killian strummed the opening of 'Southern Cross.' Sean, Declan, and Willy sang backup and harmony to Killian's lead.

Siobhan switched the stage lights to starry skies, and the image of the Southern Cross constellation.

The audience ate it up.

Killian lifted off his guitar strap and handed it to a stagehand, who exchanged it for his electric guitar.

"I dedicate this next song to a young lady with a secret desire to be a ninja." He winked at Riley, who bugged her eyes at him.

She slid down in her seat and covered her eyes.

He moved to the lip of the stage as the superfans knew what was to come. He knew how to build anticipation and stomped his foot. The audience clapped eagerly, begging him to play. The drummer kicked in a rhythmic beat. Killian raised his hand, gripping his gold pick, and yelled, "ONE, TWO, THREE, FOUR!"

A violinist appeared, playing a fast Irish jig.

Killian brought his pick down hard, rock style. He strummed fast, and assumed the countenance of a hard rock guitarist, stepping around and sliding his hand up and down the neck, moving it back and forth and strumming down in a long reach. What began as an Irish tune morphed into rock, with Killian's powerful voice singing about America.

The mostly American audience went wild.

He lifted his arms over his head to get the audience clapping. He loved it when he had them in the palm of his hand.

Another drummer appeared with an Irish bodhran drum. Killian played toward him, and they launched into another spirited song.

Killian played hard and fast, his fingers working the frets like a master, teasing the strings to reverberate. He launched into 'The National Anthem,' a la Jimi Hendrix style, knowing the baby boomers in the crowd would go crazy.

Not only did they go crazy, they gave him a standing

ovation when he ended it.

He exchanged the electric guitar for his acoustic and twisted the tuning pegs while he bantered with the audience. Strumming a country rock beat, Killian stepped to the edge of the stage.

"Here's a song I wrote, called 'Met You in My Dreams.'" He caught himself before saying this song was for the lovely American front row center.

As he sang about love through the passage of time, Riley gazed at him like he could do no wrong.

Fans gave him adoring looks all the time, but this…this woman had already blazed a pathway to his soul—as if he'd known her all his life.

This sudden realization caused him to botch a lyric. He closed his eyes to break his visual hold on her and reset his derailed train back on the tracks. He'd never experienced this kind of thing during a performance.

It threw him off his game.

His song brought the house down, the whooping and hollering at a fever pitch. He stole a glance to see Zippy form a heart with her fingers. She pointed at Riley, then at him, and touched her hand to her chest.

Message received. Clear and strong.

Time slowed when Killian realized this woman could mean a fundamental change for him. He didn't know but didn't question why. She wasn't a drop-dead gorgeous beauty as most he'd dated were, but something about her had a magnetic pull he couldn't resist.

He wouldn't overthink it. For once, he'd let his heart lead the way instead of his dick.

And only time would tell.

Chapter 16

Riley

Riley invited Zippy to walk with her to the VIP suite because Zippy was curious where it was. After the show, Riley decided not to change from the lavender sundress Zippy had loaned her, with spaghetti straps tied on top of her shoulders.

"I have to say, Rye," Zippy invoked her philosophical tone. "Loverboy looked at you the whole time he sang the song he wrote. I don't mean to say—well, yes, I do. I saw a guy who's really into you. In fact, I'll bet a fleet of cruise ships he wrote it for you."

Riley guffawed. "Give me a break, Zip. We've only known each other for a few days. Seventy-two hours, to be exact. How would he have time to write a song for my benefit? How many umbrella drinks have you had tonight, anyway?"

She laughed and drew back to look at her friend.

"I'm serious," said Zippy. "Ask him about it. See what he says."

"Yeah, right? I'll ask him and make a fool of myself," snorted Riley.

The women approached a large teak door with a key-card reader on the wall next to it. Zippy turned to her. "I'm beyond excited for you. And for me too. I'm meeting Sean later. Wish me luck."

She jumped her brows at Riley, who laughed.

"You, of all people, don't need luck with men. You're a man-magnet." Riley gave her friend a spontaneous hug. "Thanks so much for talking me into doing all this."

"I knew once I got you here, I could get you to come out of yourself. You've grown by leaps and bounds over the past several days," said Zippy. "Take the girl out of Seattle, send her to the Caribbean, and magic happens."

The door opened, and Killian stuck his head out.

"Hello, ladies," he said, opening the door wider. He still wore his white shirt and pants from the show, and it caused Riley's breath to catch.

Zippy gave him a fast down-and-up assessment, motioning with her hands like a fashion designer. "This whole Michael the Archangel vibe you have going on works for you. Just saying.'"

Killian broke out in an amused smile. "Another lass who can give the craic."

Zippy's brows shot up. "Not sure what that is, but I'll take it as a compliment." She looked Killian square in the eye. "I need to say this because Riley is the closest thing I have to family. For your sake, I hope your intentions are sincere and you aren't messing with Riley's feelings. Because if you are, trust me, honey—I will come for you. And my revenge will be swift." Zippy made a V with her fingers and pointed them at her eyes, then at Killian. "Capeesh?"

Riley's eyes widened along with his.

Killian stood still as a standing stone. "Understood."

Zippy turned to Riley. "Now go have fun. Don't do anything I wouldn't. See you when I see you." She winked and tossed her hair back, stilettos clicking as she stepped briskly back to the main deck.

Riley's butterflies had whipped around inside her ever since leaving the theater.

"You were fantastic tonight," she said shyly.

"Thanks. I had a good show." Killian motioned her to come inside. "It was fun tonight. Good vibes from the audience."

Riley stopped herself from blurting: *because you're unbelievably hot!* She stepped through the entrance to the VIP suites.

"These are the staterooms," he said, motioning. "We each have our own." He opened a door at the end of the corridor and made a sweeping gesture. "Welcome to my boudoir."

Riley's pulse raced, and she tingled, upon entering his personal space. His stateroom was smaller than she had imagined. She'd envisioned the VIP area to have large rooms.

"This is nice, but you don't have a private balcony," she noted.

"Not like yours. We share a private VIP one, though," he said. "Can I get you a beverage? Alcohol? Non-alcohol?"

He opened a mini-fridge. "This suite comes with a private butler. All I have to do is ask for a pint of black stuff or a bottle of whiskey, and they magically appear."

"How fitting for an Irish cruise." Riley spotted a bottle of champagne. "I'll have a glass of bubbly."

"Coming right up. Have a seat." He gripped the bottle and carefully unwound the tight wire, squinting, as if expecting the cork to explode. He wrestled it off, poured it into a glass flute, and handed it to her. "There you go."

"Another hidden talent. What can't you do?" She made herself comfortable in an armchair. No way did she want to appear presumptuous by sitting on his bed, especially after being forward with him last night.

"Not good at keeping people happy, I'm afraid." He poured himself half a flute and sat on his bed, across from her.

Riley did a double take. "Why would you say such a thing? You make millions happy with your music." She gave him a coy smile. "And with other things when you're only in your kilt."

Killian chuckled. "Ah yes, bare man's chest. Forever a crowd pleaser."

"In case you're wondering, I like you for your brains more than your body," she said, lifting her glass. She had to admit it was partly true.

"Thank you, Miss Riley." He lifted his flute. "What'll we toast?"

Riley considered a minute. "Defective luggage. I wouldn't have met you had it not been for my intimates raining down on you."

Killian's spontaneous laugh tickled her. He clinked her glass, and they sipped, his dark eyes reminding her of something ancient and mysterious.

Those gentle eyes studied her. "Doesn't matter. I would have found my way to you."

Her heart soared to the Southern Cross constellation. At this rate, it would never make its way back, nor did she care.

"Leave it to a songwriter to say such a sentiment."
Did he mean it?

"I'm not feeding you a load of bollocks. I meant every word."

Her brows rose in surprise. "It's just—you've come onto me so fast since meeting you. You're rolling at supersonic speed." She gave him a curious look. "No one does this to *me*. Did you take me to dinner on a bet? I've seen the hot-guy-dates-geek movies. You can be honest."

"Why would you say that? You consider yourself a geek?" He looked at her as if she'd sprouted gills and scales. "You're here with me because I like you and want to spend time with you. Time is precious. We can't afford to waste it."

He said that before…but when? No, impossible.

"I agree. We can't afford to squander time," she responded.

And I've said this to him before. Also, impossible.

She downed her champagne and held out her flute, glancing around his room. She didn't see much that was his.

Killian refilled her glass. "Don't drink it all at once," he cautioned, watching her sip.

Riley swung her gaze back to him, inhaling every detail so she could lock them into her memory: How he only had one dimple on his right cheek when he smiled; his straight, white teeth and wheat-colored hair, reminding her of beach sand. The broad shoulders and narrow hips. One glorious mass of brawny masculinity.

"What are you gandering at?" His roguish eyes darted around, faking suspicion.

She snapped out of her carnal appraisal. "I was, uh…thinking how odd it is to see you wearing more than your kilt."

"I wear nothing under it," he said casually, his face full of mischief.

"One myth dispelled, then." She subconsciously licked her bottom lip, envisioning it.

"Tell me what you do for a living." He poured more champagne.

"Don't want to discuss real life. I'm here to forget mine."

"Can't be that bad, can it? Unless you're a ditch digger."

"I'm a technical writer. Have you ever ordered a piece of furniture or a light fixture and had to assemble it? Chances are you've read directions I've written."

He drew back, surprised. "Seriously? Don't the people who make this stuff write how to assemble it?"

Riley swirled the bubbly in her glass and stared at it. "You would think. But I make good money writing it for them." She heaved out a sigh. "I don't know if I'll have a job when I get back. My boss didn't want me to take time off."

"Why not?"

"He thinks every writing contract is a life-or-death proposition."

"You must be good at what you do," said Killian. "He must not want to lose you."

"No, he's paranoid I won't return from vacation. Told him I was going, grabbed my stuff, and marched out of my office."

"Good on you, lass." His brown eyes sparkled. "But if you had your druthers, what would you do?"

"Write books. And poetry. I have heaps of notebooks with poems, but I don't share my poetry. Not a fan of reading it at coffeehouses."

He set his glass on a table, studying her. She'd give anything to know what cycled through his lovely brain.

"Ever write songs? It's poetry set to music." He reached for a green laptop on a table, racing his fingers over the keyboard.

"You're a fast typist for a stripper," she teased, watching his hands fly over the keys.

Killian's mouth twitched with amusement. "My mum forced me to take typing in high school to get a job in her office."

"I can't picture you in an office." She held her flute out for a refill.

"I didn't last long." He poured more of the bubbly and held his glass out to hers. "Here's to stripping. Pays the bills. But I'd rather write songs."

She laughed and clinked his glass. "Sometimes I read lyrics to songs where the prose is beautiful. Unlike my mom's generation with all the walrus and egg man stuff. Songwriters were on a weird acid trip back then if you ask me."

Killian chuckled. "I like The Beatles. We've played their songs in our shows." He tapped keys and scrolled. "Here's a song I'm working on. I'm better at melody and harmonies than I am at lyrics. I could use a little help." He pushed the laptop over to her, and she set it in her lap to read them.

His prose was superb. She didn't want to stop reading, yet there were other things she'd rather be doing with him. Not to mention she couldn't concentrate with him sitting so close. His heat messed up what logic remained in her starstruck brain.

She scrolled, noting a title, 'Met You in My Dreams.' There were several more verses than what he'd sung earlier in the show. The words jumped off the page at her. Sentiments she'd been feeling but didn't know how to express. A strong déjà vu washed over her. Having done this before. Having read this song before.

But how could I?

She handed the laptop to him and pointed at the song title. "When did you write this?"

He smiled, closed the laptop, and set it aside.

"Wrote most of it a few years ago. What I sang tonight I wrote after I met you." He studied her intently and her face heated.

"You did?" Riley's hand flew to her cheek, and her neck prickled; she couldn't believe her ears. "It's beautiful. You sang about falling in love with someone in your dreams before meeting them. I mean, how did you…?" she trailed off with her mouth open.

He steadied his gaze on her. "Feels like we've met before. That first day on the stairs…I thought I knew you from somewhere. Figured I probably saw you at one of our other shows. But I couldn't shake the feeling I knew you."

"I had the same feeling!" blurted Riley. "Like I knew you too. Only I'd know if I'd met you before. Weird, huh?"

She downed the rest of her champagne, trying not to overthink the coincidence. She let the bubbles permeate her system and loved being here with Killian. It was like being with an old, comfortable friend.

She thought of something she'd been wanting to ask.

"Also, the first day, in the elevator, when the lady asked if we were on our honeymoon…why did you say yes? You didn't even know me."

"I enjoy messing with people. Besides…" He gave her a mischievous grin. "I've not been on a honeymoon. But if I were, I'd spend it with the owner of the sexy pink thong."

"You would?" Riley's breath hitched, and she closed her eyes. "Oh gosh, I'm still embarrassed about that."

"Don't be. It was a turn-on for me." Killian glanced around. "Hey, I've an idea. Let's get some air on the VIP deck." He stood and grabbed the champagne bottle. "Follow me, Thong Woman."

"You'll never let me live that one down, will you?"

"Nope!" he tossed over his shoulder, leading the way.

Her heart thundered as she followed, hoping one thing would lead to another…and another…she'd been prepping herself when and if the time came, she'd give herself over to him completely…she'd let him do whatever he wanted. Her fears had paralyzed her in the past when deciding whether to deepen relationships.

Her gut told her not to do that with Killian.

Quite the opposite: he was like a drug. She wanted to do *everything* with him. After all, she reasoned…*I'm on a fabulous cruise with this amazing, gorgeous man. What if this never happens again? Seize the day. Seize the seas. Dang, this bubbly is doing weird things to my head…*

The champagne had made her giddy and lightheaded, and the sense of freedom exhilarated and energized her.

This felt like she was about to lose her virginity a second time. Frankly, the first time wasn't memorable. But tonight would engrave her memory forever. Because this time, in this place, with Killian would be remarkable.

Even if we go our separate ways after this cruise.

Chapter 17

Riley

Riley followed Killian through a dining room and out a door leading to the VIP deck. A walled-off barrier ensured no unexpected guests would pop in for a visit. Once outside, he led her over to a covered cabana overlooking silvery seas lit by a quiet moon. Sounds of swishing water and the steady hum of the ship's engines soothed her.

She stepped up to the cabana, removed her sandals, and sunk into a wide chaise lounge. Killian plopped beside her. He handed her the champagne bottle.

"We'll pass this back and forth since we've already swapped spit."

"Yes, we have." Riley smiled and took a swig, careful not to dribble it onto her sundress. "What is your schedule after this cruise? Going back to Vegas?"

Killian shook his head. "Rex wants to book us on another cruise, but I'm not a fan of being on the ocean. It's why me and the boys liked Vegas. At least I knew where I was when I woke in the morning. Irish Thunder's production costs increased on the strip, so now Rex wants us to increase revenue but doing these cruises."

Riley nodded. "I've heard touring is hard."

"Hard on everything. Families, personal life…" He glanced at her. "Relationships."

"Can't you tell your manager you don't want to tour?"

"I wish that's how it worked. He's our boss and tells *us*." Killian took another swig from the bottle.

"Tell me about Ireland." Riley hoped she wouldn't regret this bubbly in the morning.

"Have you ever been?"

"No. I want to go more than anything, but it's never materialized. Like every other American, I want to search for my relatives."

"Researching ancestry is a lucrative business in Ireland these days." Killian reached over and placed his hand on hers. "I could take you there."

His sudden offer caught her off guard, and a flurry of butterflies fluttered her stomach.

"I'm not—I don't know if I could get time off to go," she stuttered.

"Is that the real reason, or are you afraid?" He posed the question innocently enough, but it rankled her.

"Afraid of what? I'm not afraid of anything," she lied.

How does he know this about me?

She thought she'd disguised her insecurities with her brave new devil-may-care attitude.

"If you want something bad enough, you'll find a way to get it."

"Some of us can't afford it. I'm not a rich entertainer. I'm not worldly, like you." She said it snottier than she meant to, but he'd pushed a sensitive button.

Killian stared out at the water. "So that's it, is it?"

Regret washed over her. "Sorry, didn't mean to snark. I came here to escape my life…" she trailed off, shaking her head.

"You're worldly enough. Stop judging yourself." He lifted his arm and stretched it around her, his hand warm on her bare shoulder. "I can help you escape," he said in a low sexy tone.

She leaned into his body heat, his touch intoxicating her.

This time Riley waited for him to kiss her, and he didn't disappoint. He was right there, not wasting time. She melded into him, yielding to his touch. Their tongues danced, hungry for each other.

Her body vibrated with sensations she couldn't describe. He made her feel valued, sensual, and feminine. When he attempted to break the kiss, she pulled him closer, afraid he would go poof and disappear—as if he were too good to be true.

Killian broke the kiss and spoke against her lips. "Have to go water the seahorses. Be right back."

Reluctantly, she let go. He hopped off the cabana and disappeared through the door. Riley moved to the deck railing to observe the tranquil ocean slide past the ship. The polished teal wood felt cool to the touch, shining in the moonlight.

Riley decided she'd make love with Killian if the chance presented itself. Heck, she'd decided the second he dangled her thong from his forefinger. She couldn't tell him though—not when he said most women were only after his body and his looks. Riley admitted that at first, he'd attracted her with his looks. But after getting to know him, he wasn't at all what she'd expected. Killian possessed a graceful humility that was refreshing, and she found his lack of arrogance and unassuming nature downright erotic.

Yes, she would give herself to him if it's what they both decided. She was tired of playing it safe and wanted to live life on the edge now.

Maybe Killian was right. Maybe she was afraid.

The door opened and closed, and Riley waited for him to join her at the deck railing to take in the starry night. She was up for a vacay romance and if he invited her to his room, she'd go in a Seattle second.

Killian came up behind her and grasped her shoulders.

"Look, Riley. You do things to me I can't control. We don't know what tomorrow will bring." He turned her around to face him. "I want you. And I think you want me. At least I hope you do. If so, will you let me take you?" His eyes were hooded with an urgent desire.

"Yes. I've already decided," she whispered. "Take me, Killian." She rivaled his urgency with her own need.

Riley unbuttoned his shirt and slipped her hand inside, while he tugged at the tied spaghetti straps on her shoulders. They came undone quickly and easily. The top of her dress sagged, exposing her cleavage. He moved his lips around the base of her throat and skimmed her décolletage while his hand found one bare breast, then the other.

Riley sucked in a breath and finished unbuttoning his shirt. She pushed it off his shoulders, loving his bulk. Every delectable inch of his fine body deserved to be touched, and she smoothed her palms over his pecs and abdomen.

"You work out, don't you?"

"Have to," he breathed. He moved his mouth to her breast. "For the show."

Her head fell back, and she wanted him to consume

her. She lifted her leg and wrapped it around his, rubbing the length of his leg with her foot. "You make me feel like a goddess."

"You *are*. You're my pink thong goddess."

This was erotic as hell on this starry night, in a sea renowned for romance. He suckled her breasts, and she watched him, appreciating how gentle he was—how turned on he was. By *her*.

She wanted him. *Now.*

He lifted his head, scooped her into his arms, and carried her to the secluded cabana. When he set her down, she lifted her dress high on her thighs. She wanted him more than she'd ever wanted anything.

Killian held up a flat packet and lowered his face to hers, eyes glittering in the moonlight. "Are you sure about this?"

"Absolutely."

"Hoping you'd say that." He lifted himself over her, kissing her neck.

She reached down to massage him over his pants, and he moaned. His hand met hers as he fumbled for his zipper.

A door slammed and a sharp female voice pierced the night. "Killian! I know you're out here!"

Riley sucked in a breath as Killian jerked himself upright.

"Oh grand, just fantastic," he muttered thickly. He pushed off the cabana and walked toward the door. "Shite, Mariah, stop sticking your nose where it doesn't belong. Get out of here!" His vexation was clear.

"I have a right to be here. It's my private deck too," she quipped.

"Leave, Mariah. Or I swear to God, I'll say things

we'll both regret." Killian's tone was level but firm, and Riley sensed he controlled his anger, though she didn't know him well enough to know for sure.

"You're with someone, aren't you? That American woman you kissed in the audience." Mariah's tone could cut glass.

"It's no business of yours. Go, Mariah. Now." Killian spoke with an unwavering, resolute tone.

During the silence that followed, Riley wondered if Mariah would march over to confront her. She stayed quiet, relying on Killian to handle the situation. This wasn't her rodeo. Riley huddled inside the cabana, hugging her knees to her chest.

Mariah erupted like Krakatoa. "Wait'll Rex hears about this!"

"Do what you do best: ruin things for everyone!" Killian shot back.

The insistent clicking of spike heels and the slamming of the door indicated Mariah's dramatic exit. Riley released her knees and relaxed.

Killian peeked into the cabana. "The wicked witch is gone. Come out, come out, wherever you are…" he mimicked the good witch from Oz.

Riley laughed. "You should steal her broom and toss it overboard." She welcomed the break in the tension. "But I really should go before your boss shows up."

Killian was right; his privacy was a rare commodity.

"I hate his wanker rules." Killian blew out air and sat next to her on the lounger. "We're both adults, right? Last time I checked."

He tugged the waistband of his pants to peek at his crotch.

Riley laughed. "O'Sullivan, you should be a

110

comedian."

"And you should go to your room. Not because I want you to, but we've a full schedule tomorrow. I need my beauty rest." Killian primped his hair, eliciting a peal of laughter from Riley.

"Is it wrong to want to strangle Mariah for interrupting us?" murmured Riley, fumbling with the straps on her dress.

"No. Everyone wants to strangle Mariah." He leaned into her, his warm breath on her shoulder.

"Here, let me help you with this."

Riley stilled as he meticulously tied the straps together over each shoulder, then squatted to help her into her sandals. "Thanks, Prince Charming. I'll leave you a glass slipper on my way out."

"Nah, just leave me your thong." He lifted his face with an apologetic grin. "I really am sorry for the rude interruption."

"Don't apologize. Not your fault."

"It was a deliberate intrusion. She knew you were here. Like an eejit, I told Sean and the boys you'd be here. We should have stayed in my room behind a locked door."

Riley spread her arms wide.

"And miss all this? No way. I must admit, though, your manager and co-workers shouldn't have a say in your private life."

"Easier said than done in my situation," said Killian.

Riley was the hypocrite now, recalling Michael's power over her because she'd allowed it.

Well, no more!

"When I'm back from this vacation, I'm telling Michael to stuff it," she said emphatically.

Killian burst out laughing. "I'd pay money to see that one."

Riley poked his luscious chest. "You should do the same with Rex. And I'd pay even more to see that."

"Well, aren't *we* a pair?" His arms wrapped around her.

She spoke plaintively. "It's time we take control of our lives. I mean, we're adults."

"Ooh, love it when you talk tough."

He gave her a tender kiss. "You're right, though. You'd better go before Mariah sics Rex on me. I wouldn't want you to experience the wrath of Rex. You know Catholic guilt? Multiply it by an exponential thousand."

"All right but remember what I said. Contrary to popular opinion, the meek do not inherit the earth. The ass-kickers do. So, blessed be the ass-kickers. Get busy and kick some, Mister Songman." Riley shocked herself by saying this and chalked it up to the bubbly pickling her brain with courage.

"Love your badass American attitude." His eyes darkened. "You're a lass who knows how to give craic."

"Not sure what that is but, when you talk Irish to me, I don't care." She slipped her arms around his neck and offered him a thong-dissolving kiss. She finish kissing him and drew back to look him in the eyes.

"You said Zippy knew how to give the craic too. What is it? An Irish blow job?"

Killian crumpled with laughter. "You're clueless, for an Irish American. Craic means you're full of humor, know how to have fun, and you give a hearty what-for to those who deserve it."

"A what-for, huh? My grandmother used to say

that." She enjoyed his compliment, and it warmed her.

Killian had indeed unleashed her inner badass. She figured it was time to act on it. She opened her mouth and ran the tip of her tongue seductively over her top and bottom lips. "Until next time, baby."

His mahogany pools darkened. "Do that once more and you won't be going anywhere." He blew out air. "You'd best go, lass."

Killian placed a hand on her shoulder and steered her through the VIP corridor and out the main entrance.

"Still up for spending the day together in Costa Maya?"

She twisted into him. "Yes. I'm looking forward to it."

"Good. I'll meet you on the pier, ten-thirty tomorrow morning. I'll be the one in the baseball cap and sunglasses."

"Ooh, you'll be slipping undercover. I'll wear my ninja outfit," she purred.

"Kinky. I like it." He lifted his brows, gold flecks glinting in the starlight. "I was hoping you'd wear a little less than that. Bring your swimsuit and wear good walking shoes."

"Where are we going?"

"It's a surprise. Sleep fast." Killian gave her a light kiss and closed the door.

Yep, this had turned out to be quite the vacation.

And no way did she want it to end.

Chapter 18

Killian

Killian showered and tossed on a tee shirt and shorts with athletic shoes for this morning's activities.

There was an insistent tap on his door, and he knew at once it was Rex. He opened it, then moved back to the scattered items on his bed.

Rex moved into the stateroom and crossed his arms. "Mariah said you had a woman with you on the VIP deck last night."

"If I did, I really don't see any problem with that." Killian heaved out an impatient sigh. Of course, she told Rex, as Killian knew she would. Mariah couldn't keep anything to herself, especially where Killian was concerned.

Rex narrowed his eyes. "You know what my policy is about such behavior. It's not professional in this type of venue. In Vegas, it was different. You could do whatever you liked off work, and no one was the wiser. Not here in this confined proximity with fans. It's not professional to mess around with your clientele."

"Wasn't messing around, Rex. Just chatting with a passenger," Killian said calmly.

"Fans aren't allowed in the VIP suite. Make sure it doesn't happen again." Rex's manner reminded Killian of a stern father admonishing a boy. As a grown man, he didn't appreciate it.

"Who I spend time with on this cruise is my business." Killian lifted his daypack over his shoulder. "Now, if you'll excuse me, I'm going onshore to do some touring."

Rex lifted his finger and shook it at him. "Giving you fair warning. We can't afford adverse publicity. Don't do anything on this cruise that isn't sanctioned by me. I'm the one who keeps your image squeaky clean and the money rolling in. Don't feck this up with your playboy shit. Keep it in your pants." Rex breezed out as fast as he'd entered.

Another tap on Killian's partially open door and Declan poked his head in. "Hey."

"Hey, Dec." Killian busied himself with gathering his stuff.

"Don't worry, the rest of us got the same bollocks. But watch your back with Mariah. She's seething over this woman you're seeing." Declan raised his hands. "Don't get me wrong. I think it's fantastic you found someone you like to spend time with. But our vindictive, scorned diva will make trouble if given the chance. It's no secret she's been working on Rex for more stage time and money, claiming she should make as much as you."

Killian rolled his eyes toward the ceiling. "So, I've been told. She lobbies for more solos and onstage time every chance she gets. I reminded her this is Irish Thunder, not Irish Woman, and at least she didn't have to strip." Killian gave Declan a lopsided grin. "She didn't like that."

"I'll bet not." Declan moved toward the door. "Just saying, be careful to watch your back where Rex and Mariah are concerned. Word is, we'll be boarding another cruise ship after this for another load of fun."

"Right away?" Killian pulled back. "No! Rex said we'd have a break after this cruise. Dec, I'm sick to death of him jacking our schedule around and putting us on ball-breaking tours again. Thought we were done with that. At least in Vegas, we woke in the same place every day."

"You're preaching to the choir, Kils. The rest of us feel the same. Just wanted to impart a wee warning about the sharks in the undercurrent." Declan leaned toward Killian. "Are you at least getting laid?"

Killian shook his head. "It's not like that. This woman is, well, different. I like her, Dec. And I mean…a lot."

Declan raised his brows. "I've not heard you talk that way since you dated the lass back in Cork. So, it's serious, then? We've only been on this boat for a few days. How serious can things be in a week?"

Killian tucked his hair up into a baseball cap and stared at his friend in the mirror. "You and Cara met and fell into instant lust. Forty-eight hours later, you married her at the Elvis Chapel while we were all sozzled on our arses. I was your best man, remember?" He laid a hand on Dec's shoulder.

Declan gave his friend a resigned look. "How could I forget? Too bad that marriage didn't last. She didn't know the meaning of fidelity."

"Sorry about that, Dec, but thanks for your concern. You've always been there for me. I'm a big boy and can handle whatever's thrown my way." Killian lifted his daypack to his shoulder. "This is the first woman who seems to like me for me. Not because I'm an entertainer."

"Hope you're right. That would be refreshing for

once, wouldn't it?" Declan grinned.

"Yes." Killian looked his friend in the eye. "I'm thirty-three, and tired of this lifestyle. I want to settle down someplace and record music. Sing for online concerts, perform in rich people's living rooms, or for their pool parties. I'm not interested in filling planet-sized rock arenas. It's not where I'm rolling, bro." He slapped Dec on the back and headed out the door.

Riley would be waiting on the pier next to the ship. He retrieved his phone and frowned at being ten minutes late. As he hurried to the ship's exit, he pondered his comments to Declan, and the life decisions he'd been avoiding. Eventually, he'd have to confront them.

But not today.

He fished his sunglasses from a pocket and snapped them open, adjusting them on his face. He tucked loose strands of hair back inside the baseball cap and pulled it low so no one would recognize him.

Today he was free to do what he wanted…with Riley.

Chapter 19

Riley

Riley hurried from her dance class to change and to toss a few things into a daypack. This morning when she awoke, the ship had already docked at the port in Costa Maya, Mexico. She couldn't move fast enough, and her entire body vibrated with excitement.

Her mind crowded with thoughts of spending the day with Killian. Riley wasn't sure what he had in mind, but when she'd checked out the shore excursions and saw there were Mayan ruins, she had an inkling.

She stepped down the ship's ramp to a long, narrow pier jutting out from the shoreline for what seemed like miles. A trolley car waited to shuttle tourists back and forth. The long pier reminded Riley of the world's longest umbilical cord. She'd brought a daypack full of anything she might need: her water bottle, swimsuit, and portable phone charger.

"Have fun, Rye! See you back on the ship!" Zippy waved as she sped off the long pier with the rowdy group of Alaskan and Californian ladies she'd befriended. She'd told Riley they intended to check out the pool lounges at the big resorts.

"Riley!" called out Killian, striding up. "Sorry for the delay. Ready for adventure?"

She hardly recognized him in his board shorts and

form-fitting tee, athletic shoes, and baseball cap pulled low over his forehead. She stayed casual as he approached, though she wanted to fling herself into his arms.

"Did you cut your hair?" Riley circled him, looking for his golden locks.

"It's all tucked inside my cap. Don't want to be recognized. Works most of the time unless some eagle-eyed fan spots me and blows my cover."

Riley laughed. "You sound like a covert ops guy. You look like one, too."

He lowered his shades and peered over them, his eyes roving her from top to bottom. "Well, *you* look Irish."

She glanced down at her green tank top, with Irish Thunder splayed across her chest. "Borrowed this from Zippy. Figured you'd appreciate it."

"You didn't buy your own?" He feigned disappointment. "I rather fancy what's under it."

Riley loved his comment but glossed over it. "Shall we walk or ride the red trolley?"

"Let's ride. We're a tad pressed for time." He put his arm around her, shepherding her to the red trolley waiting on the pier.

She couldn't remember the last time someone slipped an arm around her this way. After being on her own for so painfully long, she loved it. She boldly slipped her arm around his waist. "What do you have planned? I read about the ruins. And I'd love to snorkel. I've never done it."

"We'll remedy that. First, how about the Chacchoben Ruins? One-hour ride from here. The trolley will take us to The Native Choice office, four blocks away." He unfolded a brochure and pointed to a small map.

"Chack-CHO-ben? Did I say it correctly? I read about it at the ship's onshore excursion desk," said Riley.

"Good, because I already paid for us. We have a standing reservation."

She drew back. "Killian, I don't expect you to pay my way. Let me pay you back."

He bumped her shoulder with his. "Buy me an umbrella drink. I'll wager there's no black stuff here."

"Deal." Riley learned black stuff meant Guinness. Since she'd descended from the Irish, it embarrassed her to ask what things meant. She paid close attention when the Irish Thunder guys talked to each other, but when they talked fast with their accents in overdrive, she gave up trying to understand them.

The trolley started moving and Riley squeezed Killian's arm. "Thanks for this. I've never been to Mexico."

"You're in for a treat." The way he said it sent a trill of anticipation coursing through her.

The trolley stopped in front of a modest two-story white building fronted with windows. Everyone headed inside to check in at the registration desk for their tour. When a dozen people gathered at the desk and checked in, a tanned tour guide in a white tank top called out to the group. "Chacchoben Ruins, this way!" He pointed to a waiting van outside.

Riley and Killian scrambled into it and took the rear seats for the one-hour drive. The tour guide wearing a headset took the wheel. As he pulled away from the curb and turned onto the highway, he spoke to the group. "Chacchoben Ruins is a site off the beaten path, so you won't be encountering crowds of tourists. A unique thing you'll observe are the massive palms and other trees with Spanish moss. When we arrive, I'll explain how we'll explore the ruins."

"This is so flipping cool." Riley squeezed her tongue between her teeth—a quirk she'd had since childhood.

"I'm glad. I figured you'd like this." Killian stretched his arm across the top of their seats, and she edged toward him. His hand landed softly on her bare shoulder, and he rubbed it with his thumb, sending kinetic charges to Girl Parts Headquarters.

She toyed with placing her hand on his leg to do the same, but stopped herself—fearing if she did, they'd dissolve into a make-out session when they were here to explore an ancient culture. She kept her hands in her lap. As hot as it was outside, her arms goose-bumped from his touch.

The van followed a wide gravel road through a dense jungle of mostly palm trees. Fifty minutes later, they stopped in a sizable parking area. The first thing Riley noticed were the manicured grounds and beautiful fresh cut lawn surrounding a colossal, gray-stone structure resembling a pyramid with the top chopped off.

The group exited the van and waited for their driver and tour leader.

"Killian, look!" exclaimed Riley, fishing her phone from her pocket and snapping photos of the massive temple structure. She inhaled the sweet scent of wildflowers.

The tour guide moved to the center of the twelve-person group. "You can climb the ruins but be careful and watch your footing." He motioned to a rectangular building topped with a grayed, long grass roof. "Browse the exhibits inside. They explain the Mayan culture, and you'll understand what you're seeing. Humans occupied this area from three thousand years ago. If you want to hire a guide, you can do so at the front desk inside."

Riley glanced at Killian. "Want to hire a guide?"

He shrugged. "Do you?"

Selfish desire coaxed her into wanting Killian all to herself. She didn't want to share him with anyone. He was hers today. "Mind if we do this on our own?"

"A woman after my own heart." He unfolded his brochure and gazed up at the ruins.

"Isn't it odd how this stone temple sits in this dense jungle?" Riley approached the gray stone structure and noticed dark clouds gathering. "Let's get up there and explore before it rains."

Killian surveyed the sky. "It was clear this morning. But you're right. Lead the way."

"These are my first ruins. You should lead. You've toured ruins before, right?"

He laughed. "What do you suppose is scattered around Ireland? I've poked around more castle ruins than you could shake a Blarney Stone at. Follow me but be careful. Sometimes these places are haunted." He made a dramatic, fearful face.

Her eyes widened. "Seriously?"

"Afraid so. Poltergeists, I'm a thinkin'." He exaggerated his Irish lilt.

She gave him a playful shove. "You fibber!"

"Had you goin' there, didn't I, lass? Don't forget, we Irish are a superstitious lot." He stepped up to the first level and peered down. "Limestone. Mother Nature eroded it. Same as in Ireland."

Riley raised her phone and aimed it at him. "Killian,

turn around."

When he did, she tapped several photos. He moved up another level to a flat grassy area and peered upward. "Can't climb to the top. The limestone is too eroded." He pointed at the spot next to him. "Time for a selfie."

She clambered up and leaned sideways into him, their cheeks together. He swiveled his head and kissed her.

"Stealing kisses, you sly dog. Well, two can play this game." Her inhibitions in this ancient place evaporated and an ancient, primal urge replaced them. She removed his baseball cap and his layered, imprisoned locks fell to his shoulders, the sun glinting them gold. Holding his cap in one hand, she slid her arms around his neck and pulled him to her, kissing him for all she was worth.

Killian's response was immediate. His tongue slipped in around hers, heightening her senses. Riley refused to let anything interrupt this, not even the man who teased them from the lawn below.

"Hey, you guys, get a room!" Laughter followed his comment.

She didn't care—her insides were busy imploding. Her erotic desire became an insatiable impulse she couldn't control. She wrapped her bare leg around Killian's to urge him closer. She couldn't care less if he tore her clothes off out here in front of everybody. Her desire for him was so intense that her body shuddered with a wild, unrestrained passion that burned inside her.

The coming storm, the electricity in the air, everything seemed exactly as it was back when—*back when what?*

An approaching thunderclap did its level best to

disrupt them, but only intensified Riley's eroticism. Her insistent tongue was practically down Killian's throat.

His hand slid down her back to cup her ass, pressing her hard against him—his tongue kneading hers, matching her passion.

Lightning flashed, and neon lavender encircled them, tingling Riley so forcefully she received a shock from Killian's lips. They both pulled away as the skies opened, cutting loose a deluge. Déjà vu struck, vibrating every cell in Riley's body with kinetic energy. She stood stupefied with a realization, swaying from his kiss.

I've kissed Killian on these stones before! But that was impossible.

Killian's face tilted toward the sky, and he squinted as rain splashed his skin. "Give me my cap, it's bucketing down." He took it from her and pulled it down on his head. When he took her hand, a jolt shuddered her from head to toe. He yanked his hand away. "Shite! Did you feel that? Let's get inside before we become grilled mutton."

"Yes, I felt that! Lucky we weren't killed!"

They scrambled down off the stone temple and scooted across the lawn between fat, insistent raindrops. Killian pulled the door open, and they entered the grass-topped building and stood in the foyer to dry off.

Riley noted Killian's drenched hair had fallen out of the baseball cap, dripping onto his saturated shoulders. She loved how his drenched tee shirt clung to his mouthwatering form. He looked good enough to eat with his raw and sexy manliness.

Riley breathed heavily after their sprint across the grounds. "We gave each other a shock out there. Must have been residual electricity from the lightning flashes."

"That was quite the jolt." He reached out and touched her arm. "No shock now."

"Must mean you're a shock to my system." Riley laughed, curious why their intense kiss ended up zapping each other. "Your drowned rat vibe is a far cry from your Irish Thunder one."

He ran his fingers through wet, scraggly hair. "It's my Mayan warrior look."

An odd sensation gripped Riley.

Why did he say that?

Killian took her hand and led her to the section with the Mayan exhibits. He stopped in front of a musical instruments exhibit and his jaw dropped. "Look at this. Their ancient musical instruments were trumpets, flutes, whistles, and drums. Same as home in Ireland."

"Humans aren't that different around the world," commented Riley. "Look at these clay whistles."

"Wish I could play one of these." Killian bent to study them and took photos with his phone. "Wait'll the boys see this. Says here the Mayans treated body and soul as one and expressed it in their music. Take a listen." He pressed a button on the exhibit and strains of a lonely flute played. Killian moved his head with the cadence of the music. "Isn't this calming?"

"Yes, it is." She gazed up at him.

Should I tell him that when he kissed me, I had that 'been-there-did-that-before' feeling?

Her brain whirred with indecision.

"I miss my flute. Used to play for our church. Didn't stick with it after selling my soul to the commercial music industry." His tone held a tinge of regret.

"Killian, you should play whichever instrument you want. Where's your flute?"

"Mum keeps it under my bed in Cork." He gave her a rueful smile. "Rex considers it a sissy instrument. If you notice, only females play flutes in our show."

"That's sexist!" erupted Riley as people turned and stared. She lowered her voice. "You should go back to Cork and reclaim your flute. The heck with Rex. He can't stop you from playing whatever you want." She pressed the exhibit button. Music played with clicks, drums, and a haunting, high flute melody. Riley closed her eyes, and it was as if time stood still. A familiar scene played in real time, like a movie inside her head. But she swore she was there:

Mayan warriors run along palm-strewn paths with Killian in the lead. Riley stands in Mayan dress, at the top of the Chacchoben temple, long straight hair over each bare breast, a long tan wrap slung low on her hips. She wears arm bands and a wide, blue abalone choker around her neck.

Killian is naked except for a loincloth. Black and red painted symbols adorn his face and outline the bulging pecs on his chest as he gazes up at her. She waits for him to leap up the steps, his muscled legs gleaming with sun-drenched sweat. He reaches the top and kisses her as purpled lightning flashes in the ominous skies.

Rain soaks them while they kiss in the downpour. A high priest stands before them.

"It is now time to pledge your love," he says in a language she somehow understands. After they exchange their vows in some sort of weird telepathy, the high priest announces, "You are joined together for all time."

For all time…for all time…for all time…

"Riley!" Killian's voice snapped her to the present. "You look hypnotized."

She opened her eyes, seeing Killian in the present, after being with him in an ancient past. She hadn't imagined it—she and Killian were together in the past. That's why he always seemed so familiar. *He's the Mayan warrior that runs up the stone steps to kiss me— the Jungle Man in my dreams! I've dreamed about him my whole life at this place, in Chacchoben!* The realization overwhelmed her, and she trembled.

"Killian!" she gasped, clutching his arms, staring at him, bewildered. *Should I tell him about my dreams? He'll think I'm loony tunes.*

"Are you all right? You're trembling. Did the lightning shock affect you?" Killian's concerned face alarmed her; he seemed anxious, which was out of character for him.

Her words tumbled out. "On top of the temple—I waited for you. You came to me and kissed me. There was a ritual—a ceremony—we were joined together forever. Killian, I swear it happened. It was real—I know it was!"

Killian stared at her as if she'd teleported from the Bermuda Triangle. "Did you now, lass?" he asked quietly. His sudden somber look disturbed her.

He doesn't believe me. "Didn't you feel it? Weren't you there with me at the top of the temple just now?"

He didn't answer, and instead, he stared off. "It was the music…"

"Yes, the music. You were there with me just now, right?" She searched his face. "Killian, I think we traveled back in the past. When the Maya lived here. Either we're reincarnated from that lifetime or…" She shook her head, flummoxed. "The music somehow transported us."

127

"Time to go, people!" the van driver called out to the group huddled inside the building. "Will be a soggy ride on the way back."

Killian dropped his gaze to her. "We have to go," he said in a gruff voice, taking her hand and hurrying her outside.

They stood in the rain, waiting to board the van.

Riley still reeled from what happened inside. She noted a dark shift in Killian's behavior, and it concerned her. She wanted to talk to him about what happened, but not in front of all these people.

"Hey Irish guy, are you feeling okay?" She made a lighthearted attempt at normalcy, when all she wanted was to run into the jungle to be alone with Killian and talk about what she experienced. Not get on this stupid van with these tourists.

"I feel fine." Killian snapped himself out of wherever his mind had wandered to and broke into an amiable smile. His eyes dropped to her chest. "Wet tee shirt looks grand on you."

He didn't want to talk about it for some reason, so she didn't press. She couldn't anyway since they had to go. He seemed his normal self now, though Riley knew what happened back there was anything but normal. More like paranormal.

She hadn't imagined it; she'd traveled to the past and needed to know if Killian had too. But that was impossible…right? Then again stranger things have happened.

Riley peered inside the van and saw no two seats together. Annoyed, she took a seat toward the front, while Killian sat in the back of the van. It killed her to sit apart from him right now when her head was full of questions and confusion.

Once the van was full, the driver hopped in, and they were on the road back to Costa Maya. The wipers worked furiously to clear the rain as it slapped the windshield. She rested her head back, searching for a grasp on what she'd experienced while listening to the ancient music.

Her phone pinged a notification as they neared town. She pulled her moist phone from her pocket and dried it with the top of her bikini from her daypack.

A text from Killian:

—*Ever snorkel in the rain?*—

She grinned, dancing her thumbs on the miniature keyboard.

—*First time for everything*—

—*Can't wait to see you in your swimsuit. Better be a two piece (smiley face)*—

—*How 'bout I wear nothing?*—

A gif appeared, with a man repeatedly pushing his hard-on down that made his kilt stick out. Riley burst out laughing and set her phone face-down on her thigh.

The white-haired woman sitting next to her leaned in. "Couldn't help noticing you kissing Killian O'Sullivan back at the ruins. Are you two together now? Did you meet him on the cruise, or were you his girlfriend before?"

Startled, Riley stiffened from the intrusion. "What—what Killian does in his private life is his own business," she stammered. "I would appreciate it if you would please protect his privacy and keep it to yourself." She followed up with a taut smile.

The woman patted Riley's thigh. "Don't worry. Your secret is safe with me, sweetie."

Riley's chest tightened. She thought they were off the beaten path, but apparently not. For Killian's sake, she hoped nothing landed on social media or elsewhere to cause trouble with his boss. Though she considered his manager's 'no dating fans' policy absurd, she understood once Killian explained it to her. But what a shame he couldn't spend time with whomever he wanted.

Riley craned her neck to see Killian. He winked, making her relax. He was more of a celebrity than she'd realized. Out here in the real world, his life was vastly different from hers. She hoped no one else would notice them together.

She let out a nervous breath at the idea of getting into deep water to go snorkeling. Killian had assured her he would school her through the process, and all would be fine.

Somehow, she instinctively knew everything *would* be fine. She felt it deep in her gut. Killian didn't have to earn her confidence. She'd trusted him from the beginning, an instinctive trust, as if it had been ingrained in her—from the past? And after what she'd experienced back at the Mayan exhibit, Riley questioned everything about their connection so far. Was time travel really possible? Or had she been so caught up in the moment that she'd disappeared into her own imaginary life with Killian long ago?

That was real, right? I was back in the past as sure as I'm sitting in this van. I'm not going crazy, am I? Did the lightning mess with my brain or something?

She wanted to go back, return to the exhibit to see if it would happen again. And she wanted Killian to go with her. For now, she'd do what Killian had planned.

He was excited to share the day with her and she didn't want to ruin it for him with her whacked out head trip.

For now, she'd trust Killian's sincerity and his assurances she'd be okay in the ocean, swimming by his side. Whenever she was with him, she felt safe and comfortable. She loved that feeling.

But his celebrity unnerved her. She'd observed how women crushed on him wherever he went. Even walking around the exhibit, he drew gazes. Even if she were to continue involvement with Killian, their lives were polar opposites. She could never fit into his lifestyle.

She would work hard at keeping this thing with Killian on the down-low, a vacation fling. Nothing more. Good friends with benefits. She knew for her own emotional well-being this was the safest way to go—like clinging to a life raft in a tumultuous sea of desire.

I can do this.

No one would get hurt. They'd each go their own way after the cruise, move on with their separate lives, and enjoy the memory.

Chapter 20

Killian

Killian adjusted Riley's mask after telling her to spit in it and rub it around. "Your spit keeps your lens clear to see underwater." He'd started her off in Snorkel Bay, a cozy tidewater pond, to get her used to the snorkel equipment.

She'd squealed when she saw the sea turtles, and he couldn't wait to show her the rest of the undersea marine life.

What happened back at the ruins had completely freaked him out. Riley had seemed to be in a hypnotic trance while listening to the ancient Mayan music. What he didn't tell her was, yes, he too had been back in that ancient time...on top of the temple. The vision hadn't lasted long, but it had been real enough, alright. He was still processing what he'd experienced in the past—with Riley.

Killian wasn't sure why, but he couldn't talk about it yet. Maybe because the whole occurrence was just too bizarre. It had validated his recurring dreams, which freaked him out even more.

Later, he'd discuss it with Riley. But not now. Not yet. Something held him back. A fear he couldn't explain. He didn't want anything to get in the way of enjoying this day together. Time was precious.

Killian wanted Riley's first snorkel experience to be one she would forever remember. The rain subsided, and by the time Killian steered her onto the catamaran snorkel cruise, the clouds had separated. The sun warmed his bare back, and he welcomed it.

Everyone donned inflatable vests, and the captain demonstrated how to put on the mask and to insert one end of the snorkel tube into the mouth. Snorkelers moved to the stern and stepped their floppy fins down a metal stairway, grasping a railing to a platform a little under the water's surface.

The boat captain showed how to enter the water, and Killian told Riley to watch when he did it. Her eyes grew wide as Killian climbed down the ladder, and he sensed she was nervous.

"I'll hold on to you. Swim like you did in the pond. You'll get used to the ocean currents. I won't let go."

Riley gave him a thumbs up and adjusted her mask, positioning the snorkel the same way Killian had shown her. She stared at his chest, and her clear blue eyes told him she liked what she saw. He was glad for the distraction from her anxiety about being in the ocean.

Once they were in the water, Killian grasped Riley's wrists as the mild current gently carried them. They were in ten feet of water when he pointed at a stingray hiding in the sand. He didn't want to disturb it, as they could be deadly. They stayed to observe the stingray for a while, waiting for the other snorkelers to disperse. Killian then led Riley a short distance from the boat. He kept a close eye on her to observe her comfort level, before swimming any further. She seemed okay with it so far.

Gripping Riley's hand tighter, Killian kicked them over to soft coral, the long tubular fingers pointing at them. Colorful clownfish and yellow-striped fish hovered in the turquoise water. A lacy, fan-shaped growth waved in the current near the coral reef. The water wasn't as clear as he would have preferred, after the pounding rain and runoff into the ocean. Killian paused over a lionfish resting near the coral.

A school of colorful fish caught Riley's eye, and she pointed. He held her hand as they cautiously approached. The fish remained unfazed and milled around in a dazzling kaleidoscope of color. He loved that he was the first to introduce this undersea world to Riley.

After what seemed too short of a time, the boat horn called them back. Killian pulled her close, his arm firmly around her bare waist. They kicked and swam with one hand in a leisurely manner, back to the boat. Killian helped Riley take hold of the ladder into the boat, treading water and loving the sight of her perfect little ass as he waited for her to climb on board. He hoisted himself up, and once all were aboard, the skipper pointed the catamaran back to the small harbor.

On the way, he allowed Riley to take the boat's wheel. Killian noticed how the boat captain hovered disturbingly close to her as he explained how to steer through the quiet swells. A primitive, protective instinct kicked in and Killian surprised himself with an impulse to toss the captain overboard and take charge of the wheel.

After stowing their snorkel gear in the proper place on the catamaran, Killian asked her, "Want to walk around town? We have until ten p.m. to be back onboard."

"If we aren't, would it sail without us?"

He paused. It was tempting, but there would be hell

to pay. "Probably not. Rex would single-handedly prevent it."

Riley was like an excited little kid. "Oh, let's get our photo next to this monster rock with the Costa Maya sign and the cool carvings on it!" She hurried to pose by the rock, and Killian noted how unbelievably sexy and uninhibited she was in her bikini, compared to the Riley he'd met how many days ago now? He'd lost count.

A passing tourist offered to take their photo together. Killian handed the man his phone and slipped an arm around Riley.

"Thank you, sir," said Killian when the man handed back his phone.

The gentleman nodded. "You two look great together. Bet your kids are good looking." His comment caught Killian off guard, and his expression must have shown it because Riley laughed.

"Hey, you're blushing."

"Sunburn," he insisted. In all honesty, Killian hadn't minded the comment.

Riley retrieved a white lace swimsuit cover-up from her daypack. Noticing how other men had feasted their gazes on her, Killian didn't protest when she slipped it over her bikini. He surprised himself, as it wasn't his nature to be possessive. He thought of the gif he'd texted earlier and chuckled at his having wrangled a stiffy when he'd snorkeled with her.

They strolled leisurely along the sand-strewn walkways through town, stopping at booths to admire artwork and a colorful array of souvenirs. Everything from sombreros to colorful Mexican blankets were on display for tourists to browse. Palm trees were interspersed with booths and umbrellas as they strolled down Jungle Beach.

Killian had the idea of getting Riley a gift. He'd been eyeing pretty necklaces and bracelets, wondering what it was she liked. They admired flamingoes enjoying a freshwater bath when Killian spotted a jewelry shop inside of a building, and thought he'd check it out.

Damn the cost. I want to do this for her. "Let's go in here a sec. I need a gift for my mum."

"Sure," said Riley, following him inside the store.

Killian wasn't sure what he wanted, but figured he'd know when he saw it. And it didn't take long. He spotted a sterling silver abalone shell necklace in the shape of a tropical fish and motioned the saleswoman over. "May I see the fish?"

The woman took the box out and he looked it over.

Riley tapped his arm. "While you're doing that, I'm going across the street to the flip flop store. Is that okay?"

Hell yes, it was perfectly okay.

"I'll be over when I finish here," he said casually, welcoming his stroke of luck. He wanted his gift to be a surprise, so he waited until Riley exited the shop.

He smiled at the salesperson. "I'd like it engraved, please!" He printed what he wanted on a sticky the woman handed him.

"Of course, it will only take a moment," she said in a thick accent he guessed was Jamaican. She peered at him with a wide smile. "You seem familiar. Have we met?"

"No, I've never been here before. I look like a lot of people," he said dismissively, remembering his hair hanging from his cap.

When she took the necklace to the engraver in the back, he tucked his hair under his cap, annoyed he had to do this. Thoughts about what he'd experienced at the ruins cycled through his mind. When he and Riley had listened to the ancient Mayan music, and the weird flashback had occurred, he had a hard time believing what had transpired.

Had they somehow traveled back to an ancient past together? Is that why he'd had the recurring dreams of a woman standing on top of Blackwater Castle in Ireland—as he climbed up to her? Only in his dream he'd climbed a ladder up a tall stone wall.

Though the woman's face always blurred in his dreams, she was young, with chestnut hair that fell to her waist on both sides, covering bare breasts. She wore turquoise earrings and a blue abalone collar around her neck, with matching arm bands on her triceps…and a long, tan skirt. Like the paintings and sketches they'd observed at the Chacchoben visitor's center.

Had it always been Riley?

He didn't know why he thought it, much less knew it…like when he'd been compelled to write, 'Met You in My Dreams,' one night after waking from one about the woman on top of the castle—which in reality must have been the Chacchoben temple—and why he had written the last verses after meeting Riley. But why was the Irish Blackwater Castle in his dream instead of the Mayan temple?

When he'd sung the song he'd written to her during the show, it seemed a mad scientist had flipped a massive switch to attract kinetic bolts of lightning, fusing them together. One of those moments in life impossible to put into words. So many weird things had occurred since he'd met Riley Sullivan. He hesitated to share his recurring dreams—she'd think him an eejit, and he didn't want that. Not with someone he'd connected with on a genuine level. Someone that he…loved? Is that what this was? Or just a brief infatuation?

I want to see her after this cruise ends.

He wasn't sure how he could pull that off with Riley all the way at the other end of the U.S. from where he'd be hanging his kilt from now on: riding the ocean blue like a wandering sailor.

The saleswoman emerged with the silver and aquamarine fish necklace. Killian roused himself back to the present and flipped it over, nodding in approval. He'd plan the right time and place to give it to Riley. It was an uncertain world, and he wanted her to remember him after the cruise ended if they never saw each other again.

He paid for the gift, tucked the tiny box safely in his daypack, and headed across the street.

Chapter 21

Riley

After a quiet dinner at a nearby resort, Riley leaned back in her chair, enjoying the relaxed ambiance of tiki torches while they dined alfresco. "Good seafood here."

Killian glanced at his phone. "We have a couple of hours before we have to be onboard. We can walk some more or head back. Your call."

"Let's get onboard, somewhere private, where we can talk. I don't feel like being around crowds of people." And she didn't. She wanted to talk to him about what they'd experienced today.

"Sounds good to me." Killian hadn't said much since leaving Chacchoben. He hadn't entertained her with the usual joking banter she'd come to appreciate about him.

They rose from the table and hopped aboard the red trolley on its way to the pier. The ride lulled Riley to doze, and she rested her head on Killian's shoulder. No sooner had she closed her eyes, he roused her. "We're here."

She climbed off the trolley with her daypack and stood on the pier, staring up the ramp to the cruise ship. "I'll board first and go to my stateroom. I want to shower and freshen up." She nudged him. "Want to hang out on *my* private balcony?"

He gave her a sly look. "I'll be there in an hour."

A tickle reverberated her spine. "And bring some of that Irish black stuff."

"Consider it done." He squeezed her hand and let go.

Riley climbed the ramp and was glad they'd boarded separately—one less hassle for Killian. Aware of the annoyances that came with celebrity, she felt protective of him now. She let herself into her room and switched on a light.

No Zippy, but Riley eyed a note on the table: *Pub crawl tonight! Stop by the Indigo later. Love, Zip XOXO*

Riley appreciated her friend's ability to create her own action wherever she went. Zippy's life was a constant party, and Riley often worried about her friend imbibing too much. But Zippy seemed to know when to stop and seldom had hangovers, which was a wonderment to Riley.

Her phone pinged. A text from Zippy:

—You have the room tonight! Bunking with the Alaska girls. C U at dance class. XOXO—

Riley's heart tugged with the knowledge that Zippy understood how special this night was to her. Tears of happiness and appreciation pooled.

—You're the best friend anyone could ever have. THANK YOU! Love you too.—

Her phone pinged right back.

—Make it count!—

"I plan on it," Riley murmured to her screen.

Nervous, but ecstatic, she stripped down and took the world's fastest shower, followed by the world's fastest blow dry. She peered in the mirror. Killian had seen her without makeup today, and it hadn't seemed to matter.

A soft knock on her door told her she had no time for makeup, let alone time to dress. She hurried to the door wrapped in a towel. "Killian?"

"Yes, it's me."

She opened the door a crack. "You're early."

"Is that a problem?"

"I'm not dressed."

"All the better." His lopsided smile fired torpedoes through her arteries. "Will you let me in, or will we chat this way for the rest of the night?"

"Wait, a sec." She closed the door and darted around in a panic. "Oh, what the heck? He saw me in a bikini today," she grumbled, and flung open the door.

"Racy outfit you have there, lass." Killian's brows lifted as his eyes roamed over her. He moved into the room, lifting a six-pack of Guinness. "Bottled will have to do, but it's best on draught."

Riley closed the door and leaned against it. "I have to get dressed."

He scanned her from top to bottom. "That's debatable."

"Oh, it is, is it?" Self-conscious, she adjusted her towel, making sure to secure it in place. She had nothing on underneath.

He glanced around. "Where's the ball of fire?"

"Zippy is partying with her friends. She won't be staying here tonight." Riley loved the sudden twinkle in his eye.

"You don't say." He opened two bottles of black stuff and offered her one.

She raised her bottle and clinked his. "To Costa Maya. *Sláinte*. Let's hang out on this private balcony that

I paid extra for. No one will barge in on us unless they leap out of the sea."

"I like the way you think, Sullivan," he said, his voice thick and masculine.

She slid the door open and stepped out.

Killian followed and stood next to her at the railing, holding his beer. Silently, they watched the ship glide from the port and set a course for Cozumel. He pointed at the starry sky. "There's the Southern Cross. It's barely noticeable this late in the fall, but it's there."

"Sing that song for me. I'll do the guitar intro." She hummed the first two bars and repeated it.

He crooned, and she joined in when he reached the chorus. They continued with the next verse until he stopped and stared at her.

"Why are you looking at me like that?" she asked.

"You're the only woman I've met who knows the words to that song." His adoring look warmed Riley to her toes. The way to this man's heart wasn't through his stomach; it was through music.

"My mother played Crosby, Stills and Nash records. I know all their songs. Want me to sing, 'Teach Your Children'?" She twirled her finger. "I also know how to operate a turntable and drop a needle onto black vinyl."

Killian gave her another adoring look. He set his beer down and stepped to her. "Remember when I said I wanted it to be special?"

She knew what *it* was. He didn't need to explain.

"Yes," she said, looking up at him. "I remember."

"I enjoyed today. You know why?" His nearness whirled her senses.

"I have a feeling you're about to tell me," she murmured. Her arousal meter had shot up to medium-high since he'd walked through the door—and it edged higher the closer he came. She loved how the breeze teased his hair, and he wasn't the least concerned about it. Not like a few vain men she'd known who freaked whenever their hair blew out of place—like her boss. For all of his celebrity and looks, Killian wasn't vain or conceited.

"I wanted you to know the real me. It's important in my line of business." He ran his palms from her shoulders down her arms, grasping her hands.

Riley figured it was time for the truth. "I worried you'd find me uninteresting. I searched internet sites to see what Irish men expect from a woman and—" She let out a long exhale. "Irish men appear to like fun, interesting women. I'm not sure whether I fit that category."

He drew her in close. "As far as fun and interesting, I said you have the craic, and I meant it. It's a compliment, by the way."

"Thank you for that. I appreciate the compliment." Her cheeks warmed.

"Do you mind if I use your shower?" asked Killian. "I didn't want to stick around my stateroom. I'm avoiding Rex."

"Does he know we were together today?"

"Don't know and don't care. I didn't wait around for a lecture in case he had."

Riley told him what the woman said earlier, in the van. "I asked her to please respect your privacy."

"I appreciate you saying that." Killian shook his head and let out a sigh. "I'm sure many people saw us. And you know what? I don't give a flying you-know-what. I'm tired of skulking around like a fugitive."

"Come on. You need to relax." Riley took his hand and led him inside the tiny bathroom. She opened a cabinet and set a clean bath towel on the counter, then stooped to find shower gel and a washcloth. When she turned back around, Killian was naked.

"Whoa! How did you do that so fast?" She laughed. "Oh right, you do it for a living—"

Killian cut her off by pulling her in for a passionate kiss while opening the shower door. He explored her mouth with his tongue, while gently steering her into the one-person shower. It was a tight fit, and he pulled the door closed.

"I've already had a shower—" she started, but he cut her off with another kiss, ignoring her protest.

His hands found the Velcro on her towel, and he tugged one end away, as if unwrapping a present. The towel dropped to the shower drain, and his foot artfully slid it aside like he was doing a dance move. His eyes took their time roving her, from top to bottom. "Cripes, Sullivan."

Killian's open-mouthed gaze drifted to her breasts. He touched them with such reverence that her heart squeezed. He lightly dragged his fingertips to the front of her, then down low to her center, tenderly pleasuring her with his fingers. The sensation was incredible, and she moaned, not wanting him to stop. When Killian had her a click short of the pinnacle up to Release Mountain, he turned on the shower. "I want to look at you, all wet and dripping." His lids lowered, and he slid a soap bar over her skin, detonating it.

Riley wanted back on the pinnacle and considered moving his hand to get her there. *Patience. Let him control this.* She rested her palms on his chest, loving the uneven terrain.

"Let's get you rinsed, lass." He aimed the spray at her, then pressed his lips to her cleavage. He stayed there, venerating her. His palms moved over her nipples, and he moved his mouth to adore them, too. "Hello, my lovelies," he murmured.

"Oh…" squeaked Riley, as he worshipped every inch of her. She slid her palm down low to touch him, loving his smooth skin as she took him in her hand. He moaned, his face buried in the side of her neck. He bent to kiss her stomach, but the shower was too small.

Riley giggled when his backside bumped the wall and she let go of him. "Just a tad awkward," she murmured, squinting as the spray hit her face. "How about I get out and you finish since I've already showered?"

"Whatever you say, lass." He brushed back his hair with those magic fingers and eased his head under the spray.

Riley stepped out, dizzy with arousal. She'd never showered with a man. Her eagerness to have him touch her made her ache in places she didn't know existed. She moved to the bed and threw the covers back, then grabbed a bottle of black stuff. When she opened the shower door to give him the beer, Killian was busy shampooing his hair, lather scudding down his stomach, legs, and—*oh my God, around an erection the size of a submarine.* Her eyes widened, and she forced her gaze upwards as she held out the bottle of beer.

"Here's some black stuff."

"This is grand, thank you." He accepted it and took a long, hard pull, not the least bit inhibited. But then, he was a stripper. Watching him swallow nearly rocketed her into the Big O all by herself.

Riley bolted from the bathroom, not wanting to summit her mountain without him. Where's the fun in *that?* She towel-dried and brushed her hair at breakneck speed, then slid the balcony door open for the moonlight to stream in. A mild ocean breeze flowed in with it as the ship hummed through the sea on the clear Caribbean night. She raced around the room in a frenzy, wondering what else to do to get ready for what she anticipated. Adrenaline kicked in. What all should she do?

Riley jerked to a stop, indecisive. Should she wait for him standing up? Sitting down? On the bed? She dove onto the bed and covered herself with the sheet, ogling Killian through the open doorway and the steamed glass as he finished his shower. This was the epitome of an erotic fantasy: leisurely gawking at an impossibly handsome, brawny man in her shower, while he lathered up with soap and shampoo. She homed in on a tat of a green and black Celtic cross on one muscled butt cheek.

After what seemed a millennium, the shower door opened and out stepped Killian, steam rushing out with him. He dried himself off and rubbed his hair with a towel.

She thought she might swoon into oblivion, watching him wrap the towel around his waist. Was that a squeak she leaked out just now?

He moved to her bed, a tender passion in his gaze. "Sorry, lass, this won't do." His sexy tone nearly undid her as he lifted the sheet off her, his nearness stoking a nascent fire in her belly.

Pulse speeding, she rested on her side facing him, her damp hair draped over her shoulder.

His brandy-colored eyes darkened with want as his gaze lingered over her. "Mother of all things holy," he whispered, bending to her. He brushed her hair back and kissed her shoulder. Invitation smoldered in his eyes.

A sense of urgency had her tugging off his towel and kneeling on the bed. She'd never been this assertive when having sex, and it felt darn good. She slid her hands up his sides, kissing his chest; loving that his breathing quickened from her touch. It was easy to lose herself in him.

He eased her back on the bed, and French kissed her long and hard, licking her tongue like an ice cream cone. Then kissed his way along her neck, working his way to pay homage to each breast. He moved lower, nibbling her sensitive stomach, and continued south, sliding his lips to her aching center.

Riley had never allowed anyone to touch this private part of herself with lips and tongue. She'd not shared this most intimate part of herself. But with Killian it seemed so natural, and she longed for him to explore her there. His tongue sent explosive shivers of need through her, driving her to a fever pitch. She cried out, "Killian, oh…oh…oh…!"

He lingered there a while, then pushed himself off of her. He ripped open a packet and rolled the contents onto himself. "I've wanted you from the second I touched your sexy pink thong. That was mother effing erotic," he growled out, easing himself on top of her.

She helped guide him to her entrance. "I've wanted you just as much. Please don't stop, whatever you do!"

"Trust me, I won't…" He set his rhythm, and she wrapped her legs around him.

"You musicians. Make. The best. Lovers…" she

panted, easing into his gentle cadence.

His pace increased and her body escalated along with his. Girl Parts Headquarters took the helm and flipped her switch to maximum overdrive.

"Killian!" she cried out as waves of pulsing bliss moved through her, stimulating every nerve ending.

He moved until he released, pressing hard on her as his body stiffened, burying his face in her shoulder. "Ahh, Sullivan."

"Stay inside. Please...stay there," she whispered, loving the joyful tear sliding across her temple and into her hair.

His heart thudded against her own as he obeyed her order, kissing her neck. He was heavy though, and she gently rolled him off her and snuggled into his side, resting her head on his chest. The rapid thumps of his heartbeat vibrated her ear, calming her. She lifted her head to kiss his heartbeat.

"Killian. Everything good? You're so quiet," she whispered.

"Better than good," he said, pulling her tight. "You have no idea."

Riley forever had trouble articulating life's critical moments—unable to say what lived in her heart. This moment wasn't any different, despite her insides teeming with happiness and passion. Inherently, she knew the words. How to express them was another story, with this tangible bond between them. She had the sudden urge to tell him everything since time began about herself, her highs, her lows, her lifetime of thoughts. Mostly she wanted to tell him about her dreams.

What if Killian rejects me or judges me if I tell him

about my recurring dreams? That I'd been dreaming about him all these years?

She'd risk it. Brushing his hair back from his forehead, she looked into his eyes and chose her words carefully. "No matter what happens, I'll never forget our time together on this cruise."

"What are you thinking will happen?" he asked, lifting her hand and kissing it. "Nothing bad, I hope."

"It's just…I've not shared with anyone the things I've shared with you," she said slowly, with measured control of the emotion she wasn't yet ready to unmask. "It's like we're kindred spirits. I know our lives are in completely different worlds—"

Killian put a finger to her lips. "Let's not fast forward this. I'm content being here with you. You're a wonderful woman, Riley. And don't let anyone have you thinking otherwise." He cupped her cheek and kissed her.

"But I need to know, whether you felt our connection at the ruins? An intense bond we had in an ancient past? When we listened to the Mayan music—did you travel to the past with me? Or did I imagine it?"

Indefinable emotion flickered in his eyes. "Tell me about it. The details."

"You came running from the jungle, like a warrior with painted designs on you, and you climbed the stone steps of the temple while I stood on top, waiting. Same as my recurring dreams. It never changes."

He said nothing for what seemed like forever.

She waited, studying the ceiling.

Killian pushed himself up and rested on his elbow, studying her. "Yes. I was there. I had the same experience. Ran through the jungle of palms and climbed up those enormous steps. You were dressed like a warrior princess. It took me forever, but I finally got up to you. Then when I kissed you, lightning flashed, and the rain poured down. A man in a sarong wearing lots of feathers chanted, performing some kind of ceremony in the downpour." He traced a finger around her cheek. "I was afraid to tell you, for fear you'd think I was loony tunes."

Riley's breath caught and she sat up, her heart speeding. "Do you think we were actually together in the past? Is that why we both experienced it? It was like a real-life flashback. The images were so vivid, so real." She gazed down at him.

He rubbed his hand slowly around her back. "When that happened this morning, other things clicked into place. Like the first night I walked offstage. I was drawn to you. I told Siobhan to give you the rose because of the overwhelming feeling I had when I met you on the staircase that first day. I had to sing the song to you. Then, I had a super strong déjà vu when Siobhan turned on the purple spotlight. It triggered visions of the lightning I'd had in my dreams. I experienced the exact same thing when we kissed on the ruins."

Water pooled in her eyes. "Me too, when we listened to the music. You're the man in my dreams, Killian. Ever since I was a kid, I've dreamed about you. I didn't realize it until Chacchoben. It seems my past and present have somehow collided."

Killian's mouth hung open as he stared off into space. He reached over and squeezed her arm. "I've written lyrics about this, feeling like I've been on some path of trajectory or propulsion, but couldn't figure out what. All the while I was moving through time to you."

"I don't know what to think. I mean, what unseen force is at work here? What are all these coincidences?" Riley's pulse quickened at the thought of some higher power orchestrating all of this.

"They aren't coincidences. That much I know." Killian sat up and pulled her close. "Something set us on a trajectory to each other."

"Killian, I'm scared," she whispered, struggling for a logical explanation. "What does this mean for us, moving forward?"

"Nothing to be scared of. We're together here, aren't we?" His tone cheered her. "Maybe we shouldn't try to read so much into it. Just take it for what it is and go with it."

"You mean just…be together?"

He laughed. "Yes, just be together. Enjoy each other. For however long that is."

She peered intently into his eyes. "It appears we've transcended time, and…some would call this destiny."

"Enough talk. I want to make love to you. For as long as we both shall…be on this ship." His Irish lilt kicked in, endearing her to him.

She lowered herself to lie beside him and cradled his face. "Make tonight last forever."

"I'll do my best, lass." He moved over her, and she slipped her tongue into his mouth. She was slow and careful with her movements, sliding her hands along his skin, tasting him, smelling him, greedy for more, because the future was uncertain. She'd lock their time together inside her heart and soul, to recall it anytime she wanted. For the first time in her life, she'd found intimacy with a man that she never thought was possible.

But that was the problem. They each had their own

lives, no matter what they did together in a past one. Killian was a popular Irish singer in an even more popular group of performers.

Her job was in Seattle. As boring as it was, still, it was how she made ends meet. She couldn't turn her back on that. She was smart enough to know the present was all she and Killian had right now. She was almost afraid to go to sleep. She didn't want to wake up and face the cold reality of where they would go from here. Her heart didn't want to face it, but her mind forced her to.

They were on a path to nowhere.

Chapter 22

Killian

Killian slipped from Riley's room just before the sun rose. He made his way to the VIP suite, and quietly entered his stateroom. The ship had reached port in Cozumel, Mexico. Irish Thunder had another onshore function with their superfans, who'd paid extra for a picnic and autograph session.

Leaving Riley had been tough—she'd looked like an angel lying there, and he'd wanted to stay and make love to her again. When he woke, he'd studied her, wishing to hell things were different, and he could see her after this cruise. He knew that wouldn't be possible unless he talked Rex into taking a break to fly to Seattle. He hated that his life had spun out of his control.

He couldn't stop thinking about their shared experience at the ruins, Riley's dreams, and his own. Something was at work here—was it a psychic telepathy from past lives to present? Had he and Riley reincarnated as different people? Had destiny—or whatever it was called—brought them together again? Whatever was at work here, he still had decisions to make.

Killian took his clothes from the closet and laid them on his unmade bed. His stomach growled, and he headed to the dining room to find the chef. He requested a vegetable omelet and hash browns, then poured himself a coffee.

Rex entered and slammed his clipboard onto the table. He dropped his digital tablet on top of it and shoved it in front of Killian. "Hope you're proud of yourself."

Killian's jaw hung open as he gaped at a close-up photo of him locked in a tight embrace with Riley, kissing in front of the ruins.

Rex's mouth formed a straight line. "I warned you, but you didn't listen. This went viral on social media. Your photo even hit Irish newspapers. Good job tarnishing Irish Thunder's reputation, Mr. Can't-Keep-It-In-Your-Pants."

Killian swiped his phone to another news site and read the headline: "'Killian O'Sullivan Hooks Up with Gold Digger on Caribbean Cruise.'" He choked on his fury. "Riley Sullivan is not a gold digger. She isn't after money or fame like the rest. Quite the opposite." The fire in his gut crawled up to his face as he fought for self-control.

"Sean pulled this same shenanigan, if you recall. Took me forever to repair Irish Thunder's image. He got that young groupie pregnant, back on our tour. She dragged his ass through court, getting him to pay her to keep quiet."

"I had nothing to do with that," said Killian through gritted teeth.

Rex slammed his fist on the table and glowered at him. "I'm not doing a Sean 2.0. Get rid of this woman! If you don't, I can easily replace you. There're lads in Ireland more than eager to get into this group. All I have to do is snap my fingers."

Killian swallowed hard and boldly met Rex's

piercing stare. "Who did this? Mariah? She trashed my reputation, so you'd hand over more of the show to her. I wouldn't be surprised if she paid someone to follow me around to take these photos."

"She didn't have to!" yelled Rex. "You know as well as I do, you're the popular front man in this show. You're who they mostly come to see."

Killian pointed a finger at him. "I took great pains not to be recognized. My private life is not yours to command. I won't be told who I can spend time with and who I can't."

"And I won't tolerate you destroying the wholesome image I worked years to attain," said Rex, punctuating every word in a low, threatening tone.

"You turned us into bloody strippers!" Killian shot back, a bridled anger in his voice. "Yeah, that's wholesome all right."

Rex's eyes flashed and his expression turned thunderous. "I had no choice but to change things when your music sales lagged! And when I did, Vegas turned out to be a helluva boon. Irish Thunder became an overnight success. I made sure the strip portion stayed classy. The new show took off like wildfire and saved everyone's bacon."

"By everyone, you mean you? It saved *your* bacon since you rake in most of the cash." Killian's accusatory words hung in the air.

Rex leaned down, invading Killian's personal space. "After the picnic, you'll tell the Seattle woman you won't see her again. Got it? Now I must sort how to fix this with the media. And that's not the only photo. There's more of you fondling each other, walking around Costa Maya."

Killian jumped to his feet. "Fondling? Back off, Rex, before I lose my shit!"

"You need to fix things with Mariah. The fans loved it when you two were together. It was a good image to project. Cast members in a love affair. Not messing around with groupies, like a drugged-up rock and roller."

"Mariah? Yeah, that'll happen. See you at the picnic." Killian had to make his exit before he decked Rex and sent him flying across the room. He stomped out of the dining room, slamming the door.

He didn't care if he woke up the entire ship.

****

Killian prepared for the second half of the Irish Thunder show and finished dressing in his kilt ensemble at intermission in the green room. One more performance after tonight.

"Have a good show, Kils," said Sean as he and Willy vanished out the door in their suit jackets and kilts.

Declan sauntered in. "Sorry you hit rough seas with Robo-Rex, the controller. Don't let him get to you. You know how he is. When things don't go his way, he shape-shifts into a crazed banshee."

Killian grunted, fiddling with the sporran that hung below his stomach. "He did sound like a wailing she-ghost, now that you mention it." He shifted his weight and ran fingers through his hair. "Dec, I've got to ask you something." He hadn't shared the dream he'd had on and off through his life. He'd kept it to himself, lest his buddies think he was one string short of a bass guitar.

Declan took a seat on a corner of the long make-up table. "Sure, fire away."

Killian blew out air, studying the ceiling like it displayed what he had to say. "Ever since I was a scrapper back in Cork, I've had these dreams."

Dec snickered. "We've all had those."

Killian chuckled and shook his head. "Not the wet variety. More of the—epic kind."

"An epic wet dream? Do tell." Mischief danced in Dec's eyes.

Killian closed his eyes to recall the images. "There's a woman. A warrior princess. She stands on top of a castle, only—now I think it was a Mayan temple."

Dec flicked his eyes to meet Killian's. "Is she naked?"

Killian squeezed his eyes closed to better frame the image. "Uh, semi-naked. Long skirt and topless, except for really long hair that covers her breasts."

"That's no fun. Change your dream and cut her hair so you can see things better." Dec stood and squirted his mouth with a sore-throat spray.

Killian's eyes snapped open. "Leave it to you to think of that. Anyway, I run through this dense jungle— with gigantic leaves like massive houseplants, and palm trees with snakes hanging off them."

"Do the snakes bite?" Dec glanced at the clock. "One minute, bro. Wrap it up."

"No, the snakes don't bite—" Killian raised his arms in frustration. "I run up stone steps to the top. She stands there and some bloke—a high priest or something— binds our wrists together and chants. I've dreamed this since I was a kid. The dream never changes."

"Not even to show her tits?" Dec stood and smoothed his jacket and kilt.

Killian rolled his eyes. "I don't know, pervert. The point is, it happened for real when Riley and I were at the Mayan ruins yesterday. We both had an experience.

Like we time-traveled—only we experienced the dream in real time—like we were actually there."

Dec gave him a disbelieving look. "Did you luck into some mushrooms or acid or something?"

"Come on, Dec, I'm serious. Both of us have dreamed about each other our whole lives—only hadn't met each other, never saw each other before. This is weirding me out, bro." He stepped close so no one else could hear. "Your mum and your Aunt Elaine interpret dreams back in Ireland and people pay them to do it. I need their take on what all this means."

"You can't figure this out? You're obviously meant to be together. If you were together in a past life, that means destiny has kicked in and you're meant to be together in this life." He said it as if explaining a math problem.

"Well, any wanker could have figured that one out." Killian shot his friend a sarcastic look. "What I want to know is, how can two people who've never met have the same movie playing in our heads all our lives?"

"There's one that I can't answer, bro." Declan heaved out a sigh. "Mum and Aunt Elaine aren't psychics, they're dream interpreters. Sounds like you need a paranormal specialist. You should have flagged one down back on the Vegas strip."

"Only one problem with that. I hadn't met Riley yet." Killian ran a hand through his hair and lowered his voice. "I looked on the Internet. Only found ghost hunters and mind readers. That's not my situation."

"Then consult a scientist—you know—one who specializes in time travel."

"Where the hell do I get one of those?" Killian's voice rose an octave and he quieted himself down. "Dec, please. Run this by your mum and Auntie Elaine. See what they say. I want their take on all this. Maybe they'll say aliens planted images in our brains. I'd accept that logic over anything else at this point."

"I have to admit, your story is way out there, dude." Declan could easily pass for an American, he was so good at talking like one. "Okay, I'll call them when I'm back onshore."

Killian snapped his gaze to Declan's. "You tell anyone about this and you're a dead man." He trusted his good friend. He wasn't worried what Dec thought; they'd been through a lot together. Killian needed help to find a logical explanation that made sense to him. And one that would make sense to Riley. She was more freaked out than he was.

Mariah spun into the green room and the mood instantly shifted to tension.

"See you onstage." Declan escaped, leaving Killian at the mercy of the show's notorious mudslinger.

"Saw you with your little gold digger," Mariah said casually, sitting and crossing her legs. The slit of her dress revealed everything up to her crotch. She obviously presumed this turned him on. *How could I have had sex with this woman?*

Adjusting his jacket, Killian spoke in a level tone with a great deal of effort. "No cause for name-calling. You'd do well not to talk about things you know nothing about."

"I planned to tell you after the cruise, but you leave me no choice. I'm pregnant, and you're the father. Congratulations," said Mariah in a matter-of-fact voice.

Stunned at her pronouncement, he spluttered. "What makes you sure I'm the father?"

"Do the math. We slept together the night before you broke up with me. Or don't you remember?" Mariah smirked. "I plan to have this baby. And you're going to pay for everything." She blew him a kiss and left the room.

Killian felt like he'd been smacked with a sledgehammer, leaving him a wee bit stunned. Mariah had made the rounds with countless hook-ups. How could *he* be the father? This was stacking up to be a life-ruiner, on top of his argument with Rex. He had to get things sorted, and fast. *How do I get a paternity test on a bloody fecking cruise ship?*

"Holy son-of-a-bollocks!" he yelled, not caring who heard. He'd have to wait until the cruise ended to prove Mariah's baby wasn't his. His head swirled with how fast his world got sucked into a black hole. His stomach felt like a piranha was gnawing on it.

Siobhan stuck her head in. "Places! Strip fast so we can wrap this thing up and go to bed." She ducked out, talking into her headset.

Killian hadn't seen Riley since leaving her bed this morning, because he was too busy with Irish Thunder's busy schedule.

And now this fecked up situation with Mariah.

It was all he could do to get through the first half of the show. He couldn't look at Riley in her seat down front. When he stole a glance, he saw the hurt on her face. Well, he'd bloody well make it up to her in the second half. If Rex was pissed now, wait'll after the show, Killian thought grimly. And he'd deal with Mariah. *Her baby can't be mine.*

After intermission, Killian stood in the wings, waiting for his cue to enter. The drums pounded, and

Irish Thunder took the stage for their sexy strip act. Killian's heart wasn't in it. The last thing he wanted was to take off his clothes for screaming women. He switched into autopilot and robotically shed all but his kilt. The usual whoops and hollers irritated him. As he prepared to head offstage to interact with the audience, instead of moving down the side aisle, he stepped to the edge of the stage in front of Riley.

He placed a hand on his heart, patting it with cartoon-like motions, blowing her kisses. She gave him a half smile and shifted in her seat.

Killian slid off the stage and slipped into his cheeky Vegas stripper routine. He shimmied his body and moved close to Riley. She wore a somber expression when he swung into a full-on lap dance, rocking his crotch back and forth and flexing biceps. He spun around and lifted his kilt, flexing his bare buns, making them dance on their own.

"Will you look at that?" yelled Zippy. "He has buns of Celtic steel!"

Riley's look of astonishment threw Killian off center; she wasn't smiling. He'd fix that in short order. When the song ended, he grasped Riley's hand and yanked her to her feet. He placed his arm behind her back and bent her back to swoon-kiss her. She didn't kiss him back. Instead, she resisted, and it surprised and alarmed him.

As the audience cheered him on, he set Riley back on her feet. Her eyes flashed and her mouth formed a straight line. Instantly, he regretted his behavior. Like a flaming eejit, he'd misplaced his anger to make Rex angry and give the finger to Mariah.

He finished the show, bemoaning his tasteless

treatment of Riley. He couldn't face her after his insipid behavior. After changing in the green room, Killian beelined for his room in the VIP suite. He flopped onto his bed with his forearm over his face, bemoaning his thoughtless actions.

He eventually calmed himself and texted Riley, hoping for cell service.

—I acted like an arse. I'm sorry. Talk later?—

His phone pinged. Good. Texts were going through on this mother fecking ship.

—No! Don't want to see you!—

Her reply felt like a slap.

Excellent job, Killian. Now you've gone and screwed up the bejaysus out of things with Riley.

Chapter 23

Riley

The next morning, Riley said little after their dance class. She'd mechanically worked through her dance steps, wishing she were more enthused. Tonight, the class would perform as part of Irish Thunder's last show, but she wasn't as excited about it as she was before.

She couldn't shake the image of Killian from her head last night. She'd seen an uncharacteristic side of him she'd not observed in the short time she'd known him. When he'd entered the stage, his unwelcome vulgarity had filled her with an uneasiness—far from the tender, loving man she'd had fun with yesterday. His rough handling when he tipped her back caught her off guard. His frenzied bizarre behavior had befuddled her, especially after their shared experiences the day and evening before. That wasn't Killian. It was someone else possessing his body.

After the show, Riley had gone straight to her stateroom, turning down Zippy's insistence to party. She'd shown Zippy the photos of The Ruins Kiss, as it was coined on social media, along with the gold digger headlines. Riley explained about the woman in the van that had commented on her being there with Killian. Was she the one who'd photographed them? Zippy had pointed out it could have been anyone.

Riley checked her phone to see repeated apology messages from Killian. She'd talk to him later. First, she needed time to sort her thoughts. Things with Killian had happened so fast she needed to slow everything down so she could think.

"Zip, want to visit the spa? I have a headache and need to relax."

"Sure, Rye." Zippy put an arm around her. "You had to expect this would eventually happen. When anyone dates a celebrity, haters trash the couple. Sad but true."

"What a weird thing to do because of a bunch of photos." Riley forced back tears. "I'm not into the vulgarity Killian was into last night. Thought he and I had something special. Especially after these past few days."

Zippy grimaced. "I have to admit, Killian acted like a jerk, practically screwing you in your seat. Maybe something happened, and he had an off night."

"He's been texting apologies," grumbled Riley, opening the door to the spa. "But I need some space before I go talk to him."

Once inside, they settled into the hot tub. Riley rested her head back, letting the jets massage her toes and back. *Why had Killian acted so strange last night? Because of the photo? Rex must have come down hard on him.*

"I'm getting out to sit in the heated stone loungers," said Riley.

"I'll go with you. This water is too hot for me," agreed Zippy, lifting herself out.

The women got out of the hot tub and wrapped the towel coverlets around them.

"I have to get me one of these in real life," said

Zippy, securing hers.

Riley settled herself in the heated stone chair, which felt yummy on her backside. Zippy arranged herself in the stone lounge chair next to hers.

"Well, look who's here," said a woman's voice on the other side of her. "Killian's groupie squeeze."

Riley turned to see Mariah in the other chair next to hers. She wanted to bolt off the chair and exit the spa.

Zippy peered around Riley, curious who had insulted her bestie. "You're the singer with the show," she said casually.

"Nice photos of you and Killian. They're everywhere online." Mariah smirked. "Women are constantly after him. He changes them like underwear."

"And you're telling me this because?" Riley didn't know what to think about Killian right now, but she didn't need any help from this woman.

Mariah stood and removed her towel cover-up. She patted her stomach. "This is Killian's baby, and we're getting married. If you know what's good for you, you'll keep your gold-digging mitts off my fiancé." She flashed her pearly whites at Riley, put on her towel, and sauntered out.

"I'm not a freaking gold digger!" Riley shouted after her. Trembling, she stage-whispered to Zippy. "What the *hell* is a gold digger?"

"It's an old expression when someone goes after another only for money," said Zippy, frowning. "My mom used to say it. Geez, what a witch."

Riley's breath shortened at the words 'Killian's baby' and she sat, stupefied.

"What the heck was *that*?" erupted Zippy. "Killian impregnated his co-worker? Isn't that a mother effing conflict of interest? An ethics violation?"

"Mariah is making that up. I don't believe her," grumbled Riley. "No way would Killian do that." She snapped her gaze up to Zippy's. "Would he?"

Zippy shrugged. "You know him better than I do. He doesn't strike me as a player. Leading someone like you on while sleeping with other women? Then again, I don't know. I mean, they live in Vegas, so there's that."

Riley let out a long breath. "If what she said is true, it would have happened long before I entered the picture." Riley didn't want to believe it. Besides, Killian would have told her, wouldn't he? They'd bared their souls on all kinds of things, so wouldn't he have said something about getting a woman pregnant? *Then again, maybe not.*

"Oh heck, Zip, I don't know what to think. I'm not savvy about the world these celebrity performers roll around in. I know nothing about the music industry or show business or any of that. I mean, who am I to judge what happens, or who messes around with who?" Riley fiddled with her bathrobe belt.

"Who do you believe?" asked Zippy.

"It's a bit premature to decide that. But Mariah doesn't strike me as an honest person. Killian mentioned she was only after him for fame and fortune." Riley hoped that's all it was, anyway. And he'd sounded like he wanted no part of it. She figured he and Mariah must have hooked up in the past, though, if they'd had a relationship. "Oh crap, maybe she really is pregnant, Zip."

"Well, let's hope you weren't just the entertainment for the entertainment," quipped Zippy out the side of her mouth.

Riley stared at her, then swung her feet to the floor. "I have to talk to Killian." She hurried to the changing room, leaving Zippy in the spa.

Killian would clear all this up.

Chapter 24

Riley

Riley frowned at the ocean when Killian didn't answer his phone. Was he avoiding her? She'd left voice messages and texts, but no response. Hopefully, it was the ship's spotty cell service.

Exasperated, she hustled to the ship's bow. As she hurried along the outside deck, black clouds on the horizon had gathered. The sea was calm now, but her stomach knotted as the ominous clouds seemed to gain on the ship. She was in no mood to experience a storm at sea.

Riley approached the VIP door when Declan stepped out, dressed in his three-piece suit for the opening of the last show.

"Hi, Riley."

She pasted on a neutral expression. "Is Killian here? I need to talk to him."

Declan hesitated. "He's gone on to the green room. You'll have to wait until after the show. The crew doesn't allow anyone backstage."

Riley's disappointed heart twisted along with her insides. "All right. Thanks."

She turned and hustled down to the theater, where Zippy stood outside the entrance. "Siobhan says we're to return to our old seats in the back. People paid extra to sit in our front seats."

"Fine. I don't care." Riley couldn't care less where she sat because she didn't want to be here in the first place. "Maybe I'll go to the Calypso Lounge instead. Don't want to stay here."

Zippy's eyes widened in alarm. "You can't! We do our Irish dance right after intermission."

"Don't want to do that either." Riley heaved out a sigh and reluctantly scooted in front of people to get into her seat in the back.

Zippy followed. "Oh no, you don't. I won't make a fool of myself all alone," she whispered as she squeezed by several people and swung into her seat.

Riley's anger had frothed on medium high since Mariah's revelation at the spa.

"Killian never mentioned Mariah and her baby. He was all lovey-dovey, sincerity, and charm—he played me, and I fell for it," Riley whispered, shaking her head.

A woman turned around. "Oh, honey, couldn't help overhearing. You're famous now. Your photo with Killian was on the front page in Ireland and the online gossip sites."

Riley's chest tightened, and she swallowed hard. "I'm having a private conversation," she snapped. *How dare this woman weigh in on my business?* She flashed Zippy a look of exasperation.

"Excuse me, ma'am," said Zippy, in her paralegal voice. "I'm Miss Sullivan's public relations manager. My client has no comment on this matter. Please mind your own business. Thank you for your cooperation."

The woman sniffed her displeasure, but at least she turned back around.

Riley elbowed her bestie. "Zip, you're a good wingwoman," she whispered.

"Damn straight," Zippy whispered back. "If you become famous, I'll be your PA handler."

Riley smiled at her friend. "Thanks. I'll remember that."

The music played, and the drums sounded to announce the show. The stage lights gleamed shades of green, with the Irish flag as a backdrop, behind an emerald mist. Riley imagined Siobhan back there working the fogger machine. She was the only one in the show who seemed genuinely concerned about Killian's welfare.

Why should I care about him now? Riley thought bitterly. Her seat tilted. A strange dizzy sensation permeated her insides.

"Did you feel that?" murmured Zippy.

Riley recalled the ominous sky. "Have you been outside? There's a storm coming."

"Oh great," groaned Zippy. "Exactly what we need on our last night."

Irish Thunder took the stage and spread out in a wide-legged stance. The men launched into a medley they hadn't yet sung on the cruise.

When Mariah entered downstage to sing a love song with Killian, Riley's stomach turned upside down. Did Killian do the one thing he said he wouldn't do—play her? Use her for his amusement during the cruise while intending to marry someone else? She had to talk to him as soon as the show ended.

Riley hated herself for buying into Killian's charm hook, line, and sinker. Believing what he said. Thinking he felt something real for her.

The entire room leaned, then leveled. Irish Thunder

continued singing, and the room tilted the other way. The storm carrying the ominous black clouds must have caught up to the ship. The first half of the show ended, and it was time for intermission.

"We go onstage in a few minutes." Zippy braced her arms on either side of her seat. "This ship is doing a rock-a-bye thing. I don't want to fall on my ass."

"Me neither." Riley watched people mill around, and some glanced at her, pointing. She imagined the gossip: *Oh look! There's the gold digger who's been chasing Killian O'Sullivan.*

Riley sensed the ship move as it encountered heavy seas. She slowed her breathing to curb her anxiety.

Zippy tapped her forearm. "Come on, time to go up there and show Killian your dance moves. Did you tell him you were doing this?"

"No, didn't tell him anything." Riley edged out of her row and walked down the aisle to the stage. She climbed the stairs and positioned herself onstage with the dance class of thirty people. She lifted her chin and pasted on a smile, as Saoirse had instructed the class before the show: "Be proud to take the stage. You practiced this routine, now deliver it to the best of your ability. But above all, have fun!"

Riley glimpsed Killian standing stage right in the wings, in his full kilt regalia. Her heart sped as the music played the introduction. She counted, saying the steps internally to herself: *One two and one two and one two and kick...one two and one two and one two and kick. Switch your feet and point, point, point, and step back.*

Riley's peripheral vision caught Killian watching her, and it strengthened her resolve not to mess up. She launched into the dance routine like a pro, with Zippy beside her. If she accomplished nothing on this cruise, at least she would nail this dance. Not only would it be a personal triumph, but she'd also glean satisfaction proving to Killian she had other talents besides sex.

When the music started, Riley counted and timed her steps the way Saoirse showed them. The stage tilted, but no one seemed to notice and continued dancing. The routine repeated, with the music rising in volume and tempo. Her favorite part was the final tap and stomp that ended with a loud percussion. Riley's arms flew up in a V to end the dance, and all dancers froze in place with their last pose.

The dance performance brought down the house. Their fellow passengers appreciated the accomplishment in learning this dance in less than a week. Saoirse told the audience how hard they'd worked to perform for them. All thirty class graduates beamed in triumph, just as the stage tilted, this time at a steeper angle. Dizziness and nausea washed over Riley as she glanced at Killian, clapping in the wings, his eyes on her. She narrowed her eyes and gave him a killer look.

When the applause subsided, Saoirse told the dancers to remain onstage for a surprise. Lively jig music played, and Irish Thunder and the four female dancers bounded out. The men wore their kilts with white shirt and jackets, hot as ever. The women wore their multicolored dance costumes, and grabbed the dance class people, twirling them around.

Sean grabbed Zippy, and Declan reached for Riley. He spun her around a few times, making her dizzy. He let go and moved on to another.

Riley came face to face with Killian, who grabbed her waist and tugged her close.

"I love you!" he yelled and twirled her.

Did he really just say that?

"Liar!" she yelled, as Killian twirled her again. She pushed him away, and he moved on to twirl the other dancers.

Killian danced his way back to her and grabbed her waist, pulling her close. "I said I love you!" he shouted, fighting for balance as the stage tilted and everyone slid sideways. Each lean of the ship tilted steeper than the last.

"Bullshit! You barely know me," she hollered, fighting to maintain her balance until the ship righted itself. Heads turned, despite the chaos of dancing mixed with the ship's rolling on the wave swells.

"I know you well enough!" he hollered back.

Her world turned topsy turvy and nothing made sense. "Oh God, I feel sick."

"That makes two of us." Killian let go of her and put a hand to his stomach.

The ship leaned toward the port side, and onstage performers scrambled to keep their balance. Riley's stomach leaned with it, and nausea pushed up. The band kept playing as if all were normal. The ship righted itself and paused before rolling to starboard.

Riley struggled for balance in her stilettos, while some dancers sprawled on the floor. She lost track of Killian as Siobhan's light board rolled onstage from the wings, as if wanting to join the dancers. Overhead, stage lights swung, and the house lights flickered.

Riley aimed to get off the stage, but another large swell caused her to tumble to the floor. Nauseous, she crawled downstage on her hands and knees to the stairs, leading to the side aisle.

Zippy bailed to the back of the theater to exit, and Riley lost track of her. Audience members were on their feet, wondering what to do.

"Riley!" Killian moved up, helping her to her feet. "Did you hear what I said?"

"Yes, but do you mean it?" This was not where she wanted a serious discussion about their relationship. Especially yelling it out on a stage full of people during rough seas.

Killian grasped her shoulders, his face an ashen gray. "Yes, I mean it. We have to talk."

"We do, but not here!" shouted Riley as the ship moved upwards and the bottom fell out of her stomach.

Killian tightened his grip on her shoulders. "Come with me. This show is over anyway." He slipped his arm around Riley, steering them toward the steps going down to the audience level.

"Take your hands off her!" Mariah rushed in and tugged Killian away, severing his hold on her.

The theater rolled, and a wave of nausea washed over Riley. "I'm going to be sick. I have to get out of here!" Holding a hand over her mouth, she wrenched herself from Killian's grip and made her way down the stairs.

The rest of Irish Thunder and the dancers continued twirling around the stage, despite the cruise ship's pitching in the rough seas.

Killian followed Riley down to audience level, grabbed her by the shoulders, and spun her around. "I need to talk to you now!" he yelled over the music.

Lights flickered and the power went out. The music stopped at the exact moment Riley lost her battle with personal restraint. "Go have your baby and fuck yourself!"

Killian froze, openmouthed, gaping at her.

Heads swiveled at Riley's outburst. The anxiety from the rolling ship, Mariah's irritating interference, and Riley's crazed loathing of Killian had spun her into a frenzy. Impulsively, she grabbed a wineglass from a woman and tossed a merlot in Killian's face.

Riley froze at seeing the dark liquid streaming down Killian's cheeks. His skin took on a greenish pallor and he jerked forward, the back of his hand to his mouth.

Riley tried to dive out of the way, but Mariah wasn't as lucky. Out spurted Killian's stomach contents, showering Mariah with man puke. Riley caught part of it, and she smelled recycled black stuff.

"What the hell! Are you insane?" spluttered Mariah, with a horrified look on her face as she swiped and shook her hands in a frenzy. She'd had her mouth open, as per usual, when Killian hurled his chunks. She clawed at her cheeks like mosquitos had attacked them, and Riley glimpsed chunks in her slimy dark hair.

Killian backed up, wiping his mouth. "I'm sorry!" he croaked out.

When Riley smelled the sour black stuff, nausea pushed up, and her own contents rushed out, slopping onto the velvety cerise carpet. She dashed up the aisle, weaving around people and beelining for the theater exit. The ship lurched, wobbling her like a drunken sailor. She staggered toward the double doors.

"Riley, I'm sorry!" Killian called after her.

All she wanted was the privacy of her stateroom. As she bailed out of the theater, Mariah yelled a string of profanities that would make a merchant marine blush.

A voice came over the ship's sound system. "This is

Captain Marc. We've encountered rough seas. Passengers and crew, please return to your staterooms at once. Stay there until further notice."

The sea's upheaval terrified Riley. Panicked tears raced down her cheeks as she hurried out with the other passengers. The elevators had stopped running. Riley made her way up to her stateroom by clinging to the stair railings and hoisting herself up, one step at a time, as the ship rolled from one side to the other. In the corridor leading to her room, she nearly vomited again when the ship tilted. Heart pounding, she prayed the ship would stay upright and on top of the waves, not under them. At long last, she reached her stateroom and banged on the door.

Zippy opened it, her face looking as bad as Riley felt. "Thank goodness you're here. Get on the bed. It's the only thing that's nailed down and won't slide across the room," she squeaked out, crawling onto hers, and curling around a pillow.

Riley made it to the bathroom in the nick of time. She flushed the rest of her stomach contents that had rushed out and wiped her mouth with a towel. She slammed the bathroom door shut and crawled onto Zippy's bed.

"Oh, man. I've never been this sick," she groaned, holding a pillow to her stomach.

Zippy's face paled. "Don't look outside. It'll freak you out."

Riley grimaced. "Well now, I *have* to look because you said that." She pushed off the bed and pulled back the curtain over the sliding glass door leading to their balcony.

Zippy was right. All Riley saw was white, churning

water. An ocean resembling a snow field. Not blue. Not even gray. The sea roared when she cracked open the door.

Blurry lights bobbed in the distance, and Riley hoped it was land. But when the ship crested, she saw it was another cruise ship, parallel to theirs. The swells were so large the other ship dropped into troughs and the lights disappeared. They reappeared when the massive ship crested on a surge of white, roiling water. The rolling, thundering waves terrified her. She slid the sliding glass door closed and latched it.

"A little rough out there," said Riley in a weak voice, zigzagging back to her bed.

"Told you not to look," mumbled Zippy, hugging her knees to her chest.

Riley climbed back onto her tilting bed. "Feels like we're in Dorothy's tornado house before it hits munchkin land. How will we sleep?"

"We won't," mumbled Zippy into her knees. She lifted her head and peered at Riley. "What's that in your hair?"

"Killian blew chunks on Mariah and some of it landed on me." Riley pulled a sticky lump from her hair and headed for the toilet to toss it in. She turned on the sink faucet and rinsed the offending tendrils, squeeze-dried them with a towel, and slunk back to her bed.

"He what?" Zippy scrunched her face as the ship leaned. "Did I hear you right? Killian got sick on you and Mariah? I heard him hollering, but I had to get out of there." She rested her forehead on her knees.

"Killian said he loved me," said Riley in a small voice. "And what did I do? Screamed at him to go have his baby and fuck himself. The music quit when I said it, so everyone in the place heard me."

Zippy's head snapped up like an alert chicken. "His baby? And he said he loved you? And you said fuck? You never say fuck." Her face contorted, and she howled with laughter.

The ship kept up its rolling motion.

"Oh, my stomach," groaned Riley, her forearm draped over her face.

"Welcome to melodrama on the high seas, ladies and gentlemen. Okay, what did Killian do when you told him to fuck himself?" Zippy laughed so hard tears rolled.

"I don't know. Everything was a shit show. I was trying to stay on my feet." Riley recalled the chaos and her nausea rushed up all over again.

"Wait a sec, back up the trolley. You said this to Killian after Spa Bitch told you she was pregnant with his baby? This is like a binge series on Netflix, 'The Strip Cruise Chronicles.'" Zippy dissolved into more laughter. She gasped for breath. "When did he get sick?"

Riley pushed words out between giggles. "When Killian yelled he loved me, Mariah charged over like a raging bull in a matador ring. I ran down the stairs, and Killian grabbed me. Mariah clawed at him, and we had a three-way wrestling match."

More hysterics from Zippy as she beat the bed with her fist. "Oh man, this is rich. Then what?" she gasped.

"I grabbed a glass of wine, threw it in Killian's face, and he spewed." Despite giggling, Riley tried to continue. "When I smelled it, I got sick."

"A regular barf-o-rama." Zippy cackled, holding her side. "Sorry I missed it!"

Riley clutched her aching sides from laughter, as the ship leaned to the other side. "Oh God, please make this stop. Please…"

"It'll be a long night. We should try for what little sleep we can get." Zippy fluffed her pillow. The ship leaned to one side and her slippery comforter slid to the floor. "This is effing insane. I want my money back!"

Riley's turn to crack up, but at this point she didn't give a flying flip about a refund. "They don't issue refunds for rough seas. Hey, I don't want to fall out of bed, Zip. I'll knock myself out."

"That's one way to get through this hella storm." Zippy flashed her friend a lopsided grin and tossed a pillow on top of the comforter on the floor. "Here, you can land on this."

A final fit of laughter ached both their stomachs. Gradually, they calmed themselves. Once Riley settled into the routine of the ship's movement, she drifted off. No recurring dreams about Killian. It was as if her heart and mind knew that things were over, and they protected her as she slept. If only they'd do the same when she was awake.

The pain of having lost Killian was more than she could bear.

Chapter 25

Killian

Killian had packed his bags and left them outside his stateroom the night before as instructed, so they could be offloaded early this morning. With all the upheaval last night he was amazed the ship's crew could find any bags to unload. He hoped his bags had been found and collected in the chaos and were on their way to his hotel.

Rex had completed plans for their next cruise, and he'd scheduled cast and crew to board another ship the day after tomorrow. In the meantime, everyone would stay at a nearby hotel.

Killian hardly slept during the previous night's rough seas back to Fort Lauderdale, and he was relieved when they'd docked at seven a.m. this morning. He couldn't wait to get off this floating bathtub. Since the captain had locked down all passengers in their staterooms, and cell service had been a no-go, Killian hadn't been able to contact Riley. He'd text her once he was on dry land.

After clearing out of his room, he wandered out to the dining room to grab a muffin. He was ravenous after his stomach contents had emptied last night. And of all people to dump them on—it had to be Riley. She obviously knew about Mariah's pregnancy, after shocking him with her baby remark. His first order of business was to order a paternity test to clear his name with Mariah's accusation. He stood next to the table, scrolling through his phone.

Sean, Declan, and Willy wandered in, each taking a seat at the table.

"Have a seat, Kils. The four of us need to take a meeting," said Declan, a serious look on his face. "But first, Sean has something to say."

All eyes went to Sean, fidgeting in his chair. He twirled a fork and seemed nervous.

"Talk to us, Sean. What's up?" asked Killian.

Sean took a deep breath and took his time exhaling, avoiding eye contact.

Killian leaned back with his arms crossed. "I'm listening."

"Mariah's baby isn't yours. It's mine," said Sean, staring at his lap.

Killian narrowed his eyes. "How do you know?"

"The day you two broke up, I slept with her. She came onto me—you know how she works it. Never could resist a beautiful woman who seduces me."

The walls rushed in at Killian, then out again. Relief mixed with sudden rage. He glared at his friend. "You're a fecking wanker for letting me take the blame." His eyes looked skyward as he fought to contain his anger. "Nah, changed my mind. You're a prick. Why did you do that?"

"I'm sorry, Kils." Sean leaned back and rubbed a hand over his face. "Rex wanted to fire me after I got the other girl pregnant a while back. I've been in the dunny with him ever since. I was afraid he'd fire me for sure this time. It was a shitty thing to do."

"Oh, you think?" Killian folded his hands and rested them on the table. "It appears you now have an obligation, my friend. What are you going to do?"

"Marry Mariah, I guess." Sean said it like he was mourning at a funeral. He looked so dejected Killian almost felt sorry for him. Almost.

"At least Mariah won't be after me anymore for my nonexistent stack of cash," mused Killian.

Declan spoke up. "That's what we wanted to discuss. We've been talking about what happened with you and Rex and the lack of control we have over our own lives—how we've wound up doing the opposite from what we originally set out to do."

Killian flicked his eyes up at Declan. "Go on."

"Don't you ever get homesick? Not only for our families or the towns where we grew up—I mean for how we used to be, when we were creative and enthusiastic, and couldn't wait to play and sing together. Don't you miss that? Because I sure do." Declan glanced around the table.

Sean and Willy nodded. Killian sat unmoving as Declan expressed the exact sentiment Killian had been thinking for a long time.

Declan went on. "Remember how we were treated like rock stars back home? We were booked to the teeth, playing gigs not only in Ireland, but Scotland and England as well. What happened to giving the Beatles some Irish competition?"

Killian nodded with a half-smile. "I miss you going on about that and us scoffing at you." He glanced at his three friends. "So, what are you saying?"

Declan leaned forward. "I propose we say feck this Irish Thunder stripper business and return to Ireland. Go back to the original band we all started. Go back to writing songs and performing the way we used to—we were our happiest doing that. The positive side is, we'll be back to our culture. Closer to family and friends who helped us get started."

"Yeah—as bloody strippers?" mumbled Killian.

Declan continued. "We abandoned those who believed in us and helped us succeed. Okay, we've experienced the bright lights of American show biz and made a shit-ton of money. But are we happy? I'm on a feckin' cruise ship, stripping off my knickers like a man toy and dragging my sorry arse to bed, knackered after every show."

Sean nodded. "I used to feel energized after we played gigs back home. Not anymore." He looked at Killian. "We're exhausted. Not to mention bored."

Declan lobbed one at Sean. "Your boredom made you a father."

"Would Mariah go for that?" Killian asked Sean. "Living in Ireland, away from the neon and glitter?"

Sean grimaced. "Probably not. Hell, she doesn't know I plan to marry her yet. I'm sorry she blamed her pregnancy on you, Killian. And sorry I was a rat bastard and let her do it."

"I won't argue with that," responded Killian. A load of anvils lifted from his shoulders.

Declan stood. "We only have a few days to decide things before we board the next cruise. What do you say, boys?"

Killian's head felt like mush after last night's histrionics and his bout with seasickness, let alone his cronies laying this heavy-duty shite on him. He had to admit he'd been avoiding his own decision about this for a long damn time.

"I need time to think about it. I'll think clearly once

I'm off this bowser."

Declan raised his brows. "We thought you'd be all over this proposal." He shot Killian a grin. "Planning to hook up with Riley?"

Killian grimaced. "She thinks I'm a langer after the Mariah bollocks. Not to mention I retched on her. She's on her way to the airport by now."

"That's my fault. I'm sorry, Kils," said Sean with a soulful look. "What can I do?"

"You mean since you caused all this? How about bending over so I can kick your arse?" Killian shook his head. "So, you're going to marry Mariah?"

"If I want to stay employed with Irish Thunder. I don't see how I can join you boys back in Ireland now that she's having my baby."

Killian stood and gave Sean a shoulder slap. "Better you than me. I can't stay pissed at you. Marrying Mariah will be punishment enough. Let's get off this tub and get a cheeseburger."

A door slammed. Rex strode in with his ever-present clipboard. "Listen up. We have a few days off, then we board the M/V Royal Clipper for another Caribbean cruise. This one will be fourteen days. So, here's the deal…" Rex explained the performance schedule without taking a breath or allowing anyone to get a word in edgewise. When he finished, he peered over his reading glasses at the solemn faces around him.

No one said anything. Declan cleared his throat and Sean toyed with a spoon.

Rex looked from one to the next. "What's wrong? Oh, yeah, last night. It was a fecking disaster, but out of our control. Storms happen. I have us staying at a hotel in Fort Lauderdale until we board our next cruise. Of course, I'll deduct your room costs from your salaries." As usual Rex acted like everyone was on board with his plans.

Killian exchanged looks with Declan. He could tell by the set of Dec's jaw his friend had made up his mind.

"Nope. Get yourself another lackey to push around." Declan plucked a wad of paper from his pocket, tore it to shreds, and slid the pieces toward Rex. "There's my contract. I'm not ungrateful, just tired of you controlling our every fecking breath. If you need me, I'll be in Galway, writing songs and playing the music we originally wrote." Declan dipped a quick nod at Killian, heaved his duffle over his shoulder, and headed out the door.

"Declan, get back here! You can't break your contract!" spluttered Rex. He stood red-faced, glaring at the pieces of paper, then zeroed in on Sean, Willy, and Killian. "Is that how the rest of you feel?"

Quiet Willy spoke up. "I'm with Declan." He dropped his own contract on the table, but instead of tearing it to bits, he poured coffee on it. "There. Voided my contract. See the rest of ya's at the hotel." He tapped his baseball cap at Sean and Killian and followed Declan out the door.

"You bet your bottom dollar I'll see you at the hotel!" Rex yelled after them. He turned to Sean and Killian. "Neither of you can walk out on this production. Not after everything I've done for this group. You lads were nothing until I came along and discovered you, brought you to America, and got you in the spotlight!"

He slammed his clipboard down on the table and placed his hands on his hips, glaring at the two men. "Killian, you're the backbone of Irish Thunder. Sean, you're his wingman. I'll double both your salaries. Do you hear me? Double them!"

Sean's eyes widened, and he shot a quick glance at Killian. "Kils?"

Killian hated to admit doubling his earnings was an attractive offer, and it tempted him. "I'll think about it, Rex. But first, I need to get off this rubber duckie, then get some sleep. See you at the hotel." He motioned to his buddy. "Come on, Sean, we have cheeseburgers to eat."

Killian grabbed his duffle, guitar, and laptop and sauntered out of the dining room, leaving Rex gaping after him.

Sean followed, and they exited the VIP suite. "Wow, I've never seen the boys stand up to Rex like that."

Killian laughed. "Sean, you should consider staying. If he doubles your salary, you'll be able to easily support a wife and a child. You should think about it. Doubling our salaries is nothing to sneeze at."

"Only one problem with that. I can't perform Irish Thunder alone." Sean shook his head.

Killian slapped his shoulder. "No worries. Rex will have us replaced in a heartbeat."

As they walked down the gangplank of the ship, Sean chuckled. "Caught a little of your hurl exchange last night in our 'show must go on' mode. Siobhan said you bolted off the stage to play Romeo, but you barfed on your Juliet. Heard Mariah jumped into the fray and caught the brunt of it, along with your lady love."

Killian rubbed a palm over his stubble. "Not one of my better nights. And she's no longer my lady love, I'm afraid."

"You need to get her back. Never saw you that happy."

"Never been that happy," mumbled Killian.

The two men headed for the ramp to exit the ship. On the way, Killian tapped Riley's number. She didn't answer. He didn't leave a message. Instead, he resigned himself to the cold fact it was unlikely he'd see her after this. Not when he had to go on another cruise ship.

The Caribbean Sea was a heck of a long way from Seattle.

Chapter 26

Riley

Riley and Zippy straggled off the cruise ship early in the morning and made their way to the baggage area. Neither had slept much the night before.

"There's our luggage." Riley pointed, yawning. The women gave their claim tickets to the porter, who handed them their bags.

Zippy lifted her phone to look at herself. "Check out the dark circles under my eyes."

Riley could barely function. "Zip, I'm too tired to fly and I don't sleep on planes. Let's get a room and change our flight to tomorrow. What do you say?"

Zippy gave her a pained look. "I want to go home. I don't want to sleep in another strange bed."

"Okay. You don't mind if I don't fly home with you today? Besides, it's only Saturday. Technically, I have one more day of vacay before work on Monday—if I have a job, that is. I found a room on my hotel app. I think I'll reserve it and get some sleep."

Riley eyed a van stopping at the curb. "I have to catch that hotel shuttle. Love you, safe travels home. Thank you for everything." Riley gave her bestie a quick hug and a peck on the cheek.

"See you in Seattle, Rye," said Zippy, waving as Riley loaded her bag in the back of the van and climbed inside.

Riley sunk into a seat and dozed. After checking in at the hotel, she rode the elevator to the tenth floor. She lugged her stuff inside the room and took a couple ibuprofen with a hefty glass of water.

Flopping onto the king-sized bed, she immediately conked out, too exhausted to dream.

****

Riley woke six hours later. Blinking away her grogginess, she pushed off the bed and shuffled to the window. The sun had set, and her stomach growled to be fed. She stripped down and showered. After toweling off, she noted her phone blinking and scooped it up.

Zippy had texted:

—*On layover at O'Hare. Waiting to board. Hope you're rested. You'll need it.*—

Riley texted her reply.

—*For what? Facing Michael on Monday?*—

Zippy texted back.

—*Yeah right, Michael on Monday LOL. C U when U get home (heart)*—

Riley hadn't told Zippy what happened with Killian at the ruins in Costa Maya. Nor did she tell her Killian turned out to be the Jungle Man in her recurring dreams. This would remain her secret, now that her heart lay in fragments after Killian's betrayal. She hoped the physical pain lodged in her chest would eventually go away. For now, it was an unwelcome constant companion.

Riley's phone pinged with another text. This one was from the hotel:

—*How about a free dinner? Come to The Conch Room around 5 p.m. Compliments of Palmview Hotel.*

Enjoy!—

Riley raised her brows. *Geez, how nice of them.*

"Sure, why not? I'll take you up on it," she said to her phone. She didn't bother texting back. Instead, she'd dress and show up in person.

She opened her bag and pulled out the aquamarine dress with the white embroidery she'd purchased on the ship. The one she wore on her first date with Killian. She hesitated.

Why punish myself with reminders? Riley recalled how Killian had looked at her when she wore this dress on the cruise. Her sense of loss was beyond tears because he'd pretended to care about her when he was to marry someone else…and wasn't honest about it. Shouldn't all relationships be based on honesty? Killian's idea of a meaningful relationship was a meaningless fling, after all.

What about their shared recurring dreams? Was all that a silly coincidence?

Killian probably lied about that too, to have sex with me.

"What the heck? I paid a small fortune for you, and you look terrific on me," she said to the dress. "Maybe I'll pick up a cutie at the bar and score a fun little romp before flying home tomorrow." She snatched the dress and wriggled into it, noting how it hit the middle of her tanned thighs. She blow-dried her hair and noticed it had grown a smidge in the Caribbean sun. Slipping into the white stilettos she'd borrowed from Zippy, she left her room and got onto the elevator.

Two older men gave her the eye as she watched the numbers light over the door as the elevator descended to the main floor.

I'm not desperate enough to pick someone up in a hotel elevator.

Riley argued with herself about going on the prowl to get back at Killian. "Then again, two can play this game," she muttered bitterly, strolling along the marble hallway to the Conch Room.

When she reached the hostess podium and gave her name, the woman smiled. "We've been expecting you."

"You have?" Riley gave her a quizzical look as the woman led her through the dimly lit lounge to a candlelit table for two in the center. Riley noted a portable stage setup for musicians and singers.

"Who's playing tonight?"

"Some local group. A server will be with you shortly."

"Thank you." The words barely left Riley's mouth when a server appeared with a glass of white wine and a bouquet of roses. She set them on the table.

She smiled at the server. "Does the hotel give wine and flowers to all its patrons?"

"Someone ordered these," responded the server, and moved to another table.

"Really? Who?" Riley glanced around the restaurant but saw no one except the bartender and a woman flirting with him at the bar. A few couples sat at tables, engrossed in conversation.

With a curious frown, she inspected the bouquet. Attached to it was a ribbon with a ring-sized box tied to it. No card. Carefully, she untied the ribbon and turned the box over. Costa Maya displayed on the bottom. She lifted the lid, revealing a sterling silver abalone shell necklace in the shape of a tropical fish. She took it from the box and held it by the chain. Candlelight glittered in the silver, and she noticed an engraving on the back:

I loved you before and I'll love you forever after.

Understanding raced through her. Gasping, she pushed to her feet and scoped the lounge. Seeing no one she knew, she hurried to the bar.

"Has a hot-looking Irishman been in here? Tan, gorgeous body, light-haired?"

The bartender grinned. "Haven't had an Irishman in here for a while. Hot or otherwise."

"Okay, thanks." It had to be Killian. Who else would give her a fish necklace from Costa Maya? He was nowhere to be seen.

Do I want to see him after he got another woman pregnant?

She strolled back to her table and bent to smell the roses. A server stepped in and set a seafood fettucine plate on the table in front of her.

"I didn't order this," she protested.

The server shrugged. "Someone did."

Something was sure going on. Riley glanced around but saw no one she knew. She couldn't eat the rest of her meal and instead sat back with her phone. The only texts were the last ones from Zippy.

The lights dimmed and the stage lights went dark. A soft familiar tenor sang the first familiar notes a cappella. Riley's heart thundered, and her hands flew to her face in disbelief.

Lights came up on Killian in his three-piece suit, singing 'A Kiss from a Rose,' eyes fixated on her. Declan, Sean, and Willy appeared, singing harmony. Their sudden appearance overwhelmed her. Tears welled, and she pressed the necklace to her chest.

Killian came off the tiny stage and moved to her,

singing about love and pain. His eyes caught and held hers. When the song ended, people applauded.

He plucked a rose from the bouquet and offered it to her. "You made me promise to sing this to you. Promise fulfilled."

Her heart somersaulted. She leapt to her feet and flung herself into his arms so fast he stumbled back.

"It had to be you. The necklace and roses gave you away, but the Riesling and the seafood clinched it. Thank you." She hugged him hard.

"Whoa, Sullivan, you're squishing me." He laughed. "Figured you'd be hungry after—well, after last night."

"How did you know I was here?"

"Sean spotted Zippy after you left, and she told him you were staying here tonight. I tracked you down and talked the boys into helping me out. The restaurant manager gave us permission to sing the one song." He pulled out a chair for himself and they both sat. "You look better than the last time I saw you."

"Yeah. About that," she said, eyeing the necklace wrapped around her fingers. She looked him in the eye. "Mariah told me you were the father of her baby and you two were getting married."

"Nope, no marriage." He shook his head emphatically. "I'm not the father, Sean is. He let everyone think I got Mariah pregnant because he thought Rex would fire him. Anyway, none of it matters now."

Riley's heart flipped a somersault and a gigantic weight lifted from her chest.

"Are you telling me the truth?"

Killian waggled his finger at Sean. "Come here and tell her, Sean."

The rest of the singers moseyed over and grouped around the small table.

"You look ravishing, Riley," said Sean. "I want to apologize for causing the ruckus between you and Killian. I was a selfish arse to let him think he was the father of Mariah's baby. But he isn't. I am. Mariah told you he was because she's always been after him."

Riley glanced at Killian, who sat nodding. She hurtled back to earth as reality washed over her like a waterfall, cleansing the bitterness she'd harbored the past twenty-four hours.

"Apology accepted." Riley scowled at Sean. "But I have to say, that was a messed-up thing to do to your good friend." She looked up at all three. "Thank you for coming here to sing for me." Her eyes drifted to Killian, who sat back, studying her with a constant smile.

"You're more than welcome," said Sean. "And now we'll leave ya's to it."

"Yep, time we hit the road," said Declan, winking. "See you later. Sooner than you think." He winked at Riley and strode toward the door.

Willy and Sean waved goodbye and followed.

Riley watched them go. "What did he mean he'll be seeing us sooner than we think?"

"I quit Irish Thunder," Killian said quietly. "We all did. Well, except Sean. He's still deciding. Now that he'll be a father and all."

Stunned, she stared at him. "You're kidding, right?"

"I'm dead serious." He gave her a close-mouthed smile.

"Did Rex fire you? Please say it wasn't because of me and the whole bad publicity thing." Riley's chest tightened at the possibility of being responsible.

He leaned close and traced the fish necklace with his finger. "I've been trying to decide for quite a while now. Had an epiphany after last night."

She looked at him with remorse. "Sorry I threw wine in your face."

Killian chuckled. "I felt seasick before the show started. The wine only sped things up. Sorry for getting sick on you. I can't say I regret Mariah catching the brunt of it."

"Seems fitting, in my humble opinion." Riley flicked her eyes up at him. "At least I didn't up-chuck all over you—though I wanted to. You were a dick the night before, with that over-the-top bump and grind thing you did—" She shimmied her shoulders. "What the heck *was* that? You acted possessed."

He stared at his lap. "Inexcusable behavior on my part. Rex laid into me yesterday morning and we had a nasty argument. Mariah told me about her pregnancy before the show. When she said the baby was mine, I lost it. Took my anger and frustration out on you. Sorry I was an arse."

She squeezed his arm. "Wish you would have told me this before."

"I tried, but my timing sucked. Will you forgive me?" His penitent expression melted her heart. And her panties.

She glanced at the necklace in her hand. "How could I not, after reading the engraving? We really did share a previous life, didn't we?" she said softly.

Killian leaned in for a soft kiss. "That day at the ruins, when we listened to the ancient Mayan music, I really did connect with you in the past. Don't you think it odd we had the same exact experience? Still can't sort whether it really happened or if it was only inside our heads."

Her heart sang at his admission. "It's all I've been thinking about. Do you think it was the lightning that did it? Jolted us back to the past?"

"Who knows? Maybe the aliens really did plant images in our brains." He peered up as if searching for spaceships.

"Anything is possible." Riley laughed, relieved that the love of her life was truly hers after all.

The way destiny had arranged it.

"I believe love transcends time across all cultures and religions," said Killian. "You and I were destined for each other—whoever we were in the past—or are now. And whoever we'll become in the future."

"That's beautiful," she breathed, gazing at him in admiration. "You should write that into a song."

He brushed her hair back behind her shoulder. "When you first told me about your recurring dreams and then your jump back to the past, it freaked me out. I couldn't wrap my head around the fact I'd experienced the exact same thing. Woke up today realizing I didn't want to lose you. So, I rounded up the boys to help me win you back."

"You can't win me back."

His face fell. "Why not?"

"You can't win back what you already have. My heart was yours the second I saw you holding my stupid thong—and my heart has been yours ever since."

"Whew." He reached inside his suit jacket and handed her an envelope. "For a second I thought this was a no-go."

Riley opened it and gaped at the flight reservations.

"Dublin? In Ireland?"

"Last I heard that's where Dublin is. Want to take a trip with me? Flight leaves tomorrow and you already have your passport."

Her jaw hung open. All she could do was stare at the tickets.

"Let's see that necklace." Killian eased it from her fingers. "I'll put this on. Turn around."

She turned her back to him and his warm breath goose-bumped her bare shoulder as he fiddled with the clasp.

"Back in Costa Maya, I thought you were buying this for your mom." She blinked back happy tears.

Killian finished clasping her necklace and gently turned her around. "And back in Costa Maya I wanted you to have this. As a token of my affection." He rested his hands on her shoulders. "Tell your boss you won't be back for another few weeks."

She barked out a laugh. "I'm probably already fired."

"No worries. I'll get you a job as a dancer in a pub," he teased. "Seriously, you impressed me with your Irish dance ability. You never mentioned taking Saoirse's class."

"Wanted to surprise you." She beamed. "Then that shitstorm happened."

He scowled and shook his head. "I'd just as soon forget about that."

Riley gave him a wicked grin and lifted the bouquet of roses. "Maybe I'll give you an Irish lap dance up in my room. Unless you'd rather go back to your hotel."

"And miss out on a grand bout of make-up sex?" He took the bouquet of roses. "No way. I plan to cover your naked body with these rose petals."

Shivers shot through Riley at the mere suggestion. "In that case, let's get out of here."

When they reached Riley's room, she switched on a lamp and dimmed it.

"Ditch those roses and make love to me," she ordered, reaching behind to undo her zipper.

They stripped each other's clothes off, then beelined for the bed. When they surfaced after a bout of lusty kissing, Riley cradled Killian's cheek, tracing the firm set of his jaw.

"Two of my dreams came true because of you. You and Ireland. The first was you, saying you loved me during that god-awful shitstorm, then you baptizing me in recycled black stuff."

"I'll never hear the end of that, will I?" He upticked his accent.

"When you speak Irish, I want to climb you like a stripper pole." She snuggled into his side, tracing lazy circles around his chest.

He swiveled his head toward her, lifting his brows. "That's all it takes? Well, in that case…*beidh grá agam duit go deo,*" he said, kissing her neck, making her writhe with desire.

"Translate…" Her breathing became heavy.

"I'll love you forever." A glimmer of moonlight crept in between the curtains, twinkling in his eyes.

No one in the universe could be happier than Riley at hearing these words. Words she never thought she'd hear. Joyful tears splashed and she let them. She opened herself to him and he took her, losing count of how many times they made love. They were both free spirits now— free to do as they pleased—for the time being, anyway.

No nagging bosses to pressure them, plus they had unfettered access to each other now.

Riley chuckled to herself. *If this is make-up sex, maybe we should argue more often.* She couldn't control her want of Killian and wakened him frequently during the night, enticing him into multiple rounds of lovemaking.

When streaks of dawn peeked through the window, Riley propped herself on an elbow gazing at the gorgeous man in her bed, smiling contentedly as he snoozed. She leaned over and kissed his forehead.

He opened his eyes. "Why aren't you sleeping?"

"I want to tell you something."

He turned toward her, stroking her cheek. "Okay."

"Since we were together in a previous life, and we're together in this one, it's fitting that we're going to Ireland."

"Yes, it is." His lids drooped. "Let's get some sleep and we can talk more later."

She wrinkled her nose. "Just one more thing. Back on the ship you said you loved me, and I lobbed an F bomb at you. I want to apologize. Can we do that one over?"

"Sure," he said looking into her eyes. "I love you, Riley Sullivan."

"And I love you back, Killian O'Sullivan. There. Now I can sleep." She kissed his cheek and rolled to her side.

He pulled her in close, and she spooned into the love of her life, who made her feel that anything was possible.

And for the first time in her life, she sincerely believed it was.

Chapter 27

Riley

"You'll never guess where I am!" Riley practically shouted into the phone to her mother. She and Killian stood waiting for their bags to glide out on the conveyor belt at Dublin Airport.

Riley's excitement bubbled over, and she couldn't stop the huge grin on her face. She'd talked to Zippy first, who had been ecstatic, punctuating every other sentence with 'I told you so!'

"Where?" Her mother's voice came at her from across the pond.

"I'm in Dublin, Mom! Ireland."

"I thought you were on the cruise ship." Her mom's confusion was understandable.

"We're done with the cruise. Zippy flew home and I met someone. He invited me to Ireland." Riley could hardly contain her excitement at long last being on Irish soil.

"What do you mean you met someone?" Her mother hollered at her dad. "Danny! Riley is with a man in Ireland!"

Killian motioned her to tap the speaker icon so he could hear.

Her dad hollered back. "What do you mean, she's with a man in Ireland? She's supposed to be on a cruise!"

"Who is he?" Mom asked haltingly. "What does he do?"

"He was the entertainment." Riley waited for the volcano eruption, but instead there was silence.

At last, her dad spoke. "Zippy said you were on one of those male stripper cruises. So, you're with a stripper?" he yelled, like no one would hear him otherwise.

Riley would have no problem hearing her dad from Mars. "He's a famous Irish musician, Dad. His name is—"

Killian lifted his brow. "Hand me your phone."

Reluctantly, she handed it over, eyes pleading with his.

He winked and smiled into the phone. "Hello, Mr. and Mrs. Sullivan? This is Killian O'Sullivan." He threw his Irish accent into full tilt and shot Riley a mischievous grin. "I'm from County Cork and met Riley on the cruise."

"What are your intentions with our daughter?" Riley rolled her eyes at how old-school her dad sounded.

"Rest assured, sir, they're honorable ones." Killian looked so hot right now talking to her dad Riley wanted to jump his bones right there in the terminal.

"That's what they all say. You've only known her a week, for cripes' sakes!" Her father's voice boomed so loudly on the phone speaker that heads swiveled towards Killian, who seemed to get a kick out of it.

"Turn off the speaker," Riley stage-whispered. She didn't want the entire airport in on this discussion. "Give me the phone."

Killian turned off the speaker but instead of handing back her phone, his mouth quirked up. "Mr. and Mrs.

Sullivan, I have something to ask. May I please have permission to marry your daughter?"

Riley almost fainted. *Did he really just freaking say that?*

Her parents' response exploded from her phone, like a dropped bomb.

Riley's breath caught. "Killian!" she choked out, eyes popping. His words stunned her with such force her hands flew up to cover her nose and mouth.

More heads turned while ecstatic tears ran down her cheeks.

Killian beamed and tugged her close while he chatted on her phone. "We married once before a long time ago, so figured we'd do it again." He held the phone away from his ear and turned it toward Riley so she could hear.

Her parents talked at the same time. "You got married a long time ago and you kept it a secret? When? How could you? Is that why you never came home to visit?" Mom sounded like she'd burst into tears. Dad sounded like a hornet's nest.

Riley snatched the phone, ecstatic. "No, no, no, Mom and Dad! Killian meant—it's hard to explain— look, I'll tell you about it later. I'll call when I get to Cork. Killian is taking me to meet his family. He'll help me research our family lineage, and I'm going to help him write songs. I plan to publish my poetry."

"Poetry? What'll you do for money?" demanded her father. "Nobody makes money from poetry."

⸺ Riley inwardly groaned. *Oh boy, here we go.*

Mom interjected. "You're marrying a stripper? What does he mean you've been married before?"

Riley made an exaggerated face at their onslaught of

questions. "I'll explain later, Mom. Gotta go. Love you both. Bye!" Stunned by Killian's incidental marriage proposal, the phone slipped from her hand. Killian laughed, catching it before it hit the floor.

"Are you flipping serious?" She threw her arms around his neck and more elated tears fell.

"Of course, I'm serious. Wouldn't tease about something like that. I'd planned to ask you on top of Blackwater Castle in County Cork. But since your parents were on the phone, I wanted their permission first." Killian beamed at her.

"What a lovely gentleman you are." A tornado of sensation swirled around Riley, just like the first time she and Killian had kissed.

"Ask me again on top of the castle! And then we can get married there—like we did on top of the temple in Chacchoben way back when."

"That can be arranged." Killian hoisted their bags from the conveyor belt and set them down. He took Riley in his arms and gave her a lengthy kiss. She was sure in the history of airport kisses, this one was the longest and most passionate.

When Killian lifted from her mouth, Riley virtually puddled to the floor with hearts and rainbows circling overhead.

He slanted a sexy gaze down at her. "I figured since we were married three thousand years ago at Chacchoben, and we've claimed to be on a honeymoon, it's time we do it for real."

"We should be careful about who we tell that to." Riley wrinkled her nose. "But shouldn't we wait until we've known each other for, you know—at least two weeks? Or maybe a month?"

"We've known each other a heckuva lot longer than that, wouldn't you say? Just not in *this* lifetime."

"Wait until I tell Zippy. She'll absolutely freak when I ask her to be my maid of honor." Riley envisioned her bestie hopping around like she'd won the lottery.

"I envy you for having a close friend like her."

She looked up at him. "If it weren't for Zippy, I wouldn't be standing here right now. She threatened me with certain death if I didn't go on the cruise. I can't wait to see where you take Irish Thunder now."

"The boys and I agreed to leave the Irish Thunder name with Rex and Sean. We'll come up with another." He grabbed the handles of the larger bags to roll them out of the terminal.

Riley's enthusiasm was explosive. A trillion happy butterflies pinged her insides. "If we write songs together, we'll be Sullivan O'Sullivan."

His eyes twinkled. "I like it, it's catchy. Maybe that'll be the name of our new band."

Riley's heart left her chest and the love in it spilled over and spun around Killian like a cocoon. "Then it's settled. I can't wait to tell Zip!"

"Let's go fetch us a train, and you can call her then." Killian took her hand and squeezed it as he led her from Dublin Airport.

Epilogue

Two months later in Ireland

The magical setting of Blackwater Castle in the village of Castletownroche, County Cork, was beyond anything Riley could ever have imagined. The castle sat on a hill overlooking the River Awbeg, and the 360-degree view of the lush countryside in southeast Ireland took her breath away.

Killian and his family had rented the castle for the wedding. He liked to joke that all of his stripping had paid off. Riley's parents and Zippy had flown across the pond, along with other friends and relatives from the USA. Killian's family had enthusiastically arranged for everyone to stay in quaint cottages on the castle grounds.

Riley's dad still grumbled about her marrying a stripper, despite Killian's winning charm and his many assurances he would do right by Riley.

Her mom chided him, "Danny, button it up and be happy for your daughter!"

Riley wanted desperately to marry Killian on top of the fifteenth century Norman Tower on one end of Blackwater Castle. But neither her parents nor Killian's grandparents were thrilled about climbing seventy-six steps up a stone spiral staircase.

So Riley and Killian happily settled for the beautiful flower garden on the castle grounds.

Killian had explained that the Norman Tower was one of the best-preserved medieval keeps in Ireland and had withstood an assault by Oliver Cromwell who'd laid siege to it back in 1650.

Last night, Riley and Killian had climbed up to the top of Norman Tower on one end of the castle. In his quest to make his wedding proposal one for Riley to remember, Killian had taken a knee on the wet stone, this time with the ring. Riley fell in love with him all over again. He hadn't been shirtless like on the temple in her dreams, on account of the breezy thunderstorms; and she wasn't in Mayan dress, but who cared? A deep sense of satisfaction and happiness overflowed inside of her.

But when purple lightning streaked the sky, turning Riley's white sundress and Killian's white shirt a shade of lavender, their souls had fused once more—three thousand years later in the twenty-first century.

"Come back in time with me," Killian had murmured as he'd kissed her, while bursts of violet flashed around them.

Both had closed their eyes, but no travel to the past this time; they stayed in the present. When Riley opened her eyes, she realized this exact moment was the culmination of all that had transpired in the past.

Staying in the present must mean our trajectory is complete. Our destiny has been fulfilled.

They'd stayed on top of the castle tower until the rain drenched them and they'd retreated, laughing their way back down the seventy-six stone steps.

Riley had wanted to spend the night with Killian, when he'd reminded her that they'd better keep peace in the valley by not raising eyebrows the night before their wedding.

Zippy had gone with Riley up to Dublin to shop for the perfect wedding dress. She'd picked out a V-neck floor-length chiffon lace dress with dainty lace cap sleeves and a teardrop opening on her back that dipped low and tied at the top. Riley loved the ivory color and had specified she wanted a more conservative appearance for this occasion.

"I'll save the sexy stuff for my wedding night," she'd purred, when Zippy had protested.

For the big day, Zippy had fixed Riley's hair in spiral curls and wove a vine of fake baby's breath through her hair.

Riley wore the engraved fish necklace Killian had given her for her 'something blue.'

Now she stood before the love of her life, holding his hands. He looked a hot million in his dark blue-and-green kilt with a white shirt and black waist jacket; just as he had when he'd performed with Irish Thunder.

Riley and Killian stood in the middle of a brilliantly colorful garden on this sunny day, with raindrops clinging to the red and yellow roses from last night's rain. Everyone Riley cared about gathered for the brief ceremony.

Killian gazed at her like she was the most beautiful woman on the planet.

They said their vows, kissed, hugged relatives, cut cake, posed for photos, and enjoyed their fantastic reception in the long castle dining hall that Killian's family had decorated. Riley appreciated the generous bouquets of wildflowers, balloons, and sparkly hanging stars from the tall ceiling that Declan and Sean had precariously hung while balancing on a rickety ladder.

Riley and Killian were both overjoyed to see Sean. Much to everyone's relief, Mariah had stayed in the U.S.

As the festivities wound down, Riley sidled up to

Killian. "Let's go up on top." She gave him a seductive look, and he enthusiastically agreed.

"In that dress?" His skepticism made her more determined.

"Hold my beer." She winked and gathered the long skirt and lifted it. She'd chosen to wear her flat white sandals just for this reason.

Killian smiled down at her. "Lead the way, Mrs. O'Sullivan."

"Ooh, I love the sound of that!" She laughed, skipping inside to ascend the stone steps.

Once on top of the tower, the newlyweds caught their breath. Riley stepped to a chest-high ledge, noting the dark, weathered stone. "I love it up here."

Killian moved to her, and they silently took in the view of the manicured lawn, lush flower gardens, and endless trees.

"One summer, I gave tours of this castle for extra cash, back when I started our band. Did you know this castle dates back ten-thousand years to the Mesolithic era?"

Riley drew back, astonished. "This is older than the Chacchoben ruins?"

Killian nodded. "Everything is ancient in Ireland—unlike the U.S. where you Americans think two hundred forty-four years is archaic."

"Okay, Mr. History Professor." Riley reached into her bra and retrieved a tiny box. "This is for you."

Killian leaned in, peering down at her cleavage. "What else you got in there?"

"Open it, silly," she said with an impatient wave. She folded her hands and held them to her mouth in anticipation.

Killian opened the box and lifted out a turquoise abalone guitar pick.

"This matches the fish necklace you gave me." Riley gazed up at him.

Killian flicked his eyes at her and smiled. "Thank you."

"There's more." Riley pointed at the box and jumped up and down, heart speeding.

He gingerly lifted a tiny silver guitar that looked like a charm for a bracelet. "It's the world's tiniest guitar."

Riley beamed. "The real deal is on order and being custom made as we speak. It's an electric Fender twelve string."

Killian's stunned expression elated her. "A Fender? Holy shite, they aren't cheap! How did you know I wanted one?"

Riley loved that she'd hit the mark. "Declan told me. I got everyone to chip in, including Mariah and Rex."

Killian shot her a look of surprise. "How'd you do that? They despise me."

"No, they don't. They envy you—you know what you want, and you're going after it. Rex even said so when Declan and I called him."

"Aw, Riley…" Killian trailed off, his voice filled with emotion. He planted a scorching thank-you kiss on her lips. He drew back a little, lips still touching hers.

"I already have what I want." He tucked the contents inside the tiny box and stashed it in his shirt pocket.

Riley was dying to tell Killian that his mother had wrapped up his flute to give him. She'd explained to his mom how he missed playing it—and promised not to breathe a word until they unwrapped presents tomorrow.

Killian pulled an envelope from his pocket and

handed it to her. "This is our honeymoon."

Riley tore it open. "Oh my God! Tickets and a hotel stay in Costa Maya!" She shrugged her shoulders in excitement.

"We're flying this time. No more cruise ships, thank you very much," teased Killian. "Our flight leaves from Dublin day after tomorrow."

"I can't wait!" Riley clapped her hands. "I'm the luckiest woman in the world."

He gave her a seductive glance. "My other gift is waiting in our wedding suite."

"But your best gift is right here." Riley brimmed with excitement. "Hang on a sec—don't move."

Killian gave her a quizzical stare while she scurried to a corner and plucked a long-stemmed red rose from the stone ledge. With great ceremony, she danced her way back to Killian and held it out.

"Sing to me."

He stared at the blossom. "How'd that get up here?"

"Declan brought it up here earlier." She raised the rose high into the air and waved it back and forth. "What does this remind you of?"

A corner of his mouth lifted, and he nodded. Ever so softly, he sang the first notes from 'A Kiss from a Rose.'

Riley listened to his golden voice, studying every square inch of him: how the setting sun tinged his hair gold; the way amber flecks sparked his dark-brown eyes. His physique smoldered her, but it was his strength of character, self-assurance, and his supreme writing and singing talents that made her fall in love with him.

And finally, their Chacchoben bond, where they'd journeyed through time from past to present and back again.

When Killian finished singing, a devious thought crept into Riley's brain. She stuck the rose stem between her teeth with a shameless come-hither look.

"Say something in Irish."

In a flash, Killian responded. He grabbed her waist with one brawny arm and leaned her back with the other. His lips began their journey in her cleavage and made their way ever so gradually up her neck to reach her lips.

"*Beidh grá agam duit go deo*," he breathed in her ear. One thing about Killian; he'd mastered the art of erotic delivery after all those years entertaining women onstage.

"Oh God—do me here—right now. I know you have nothing under that kilt." She reached under it, delighted to find she was right.

"Here? Now? I can't lay you on this cold stone."

"You don't have to." She reached under her gown, removed her lacy pink thong, and dangled it from her finger. She'd planned this and it got her the reaction she wanted.

"It's the same one!" Killian laughed. He snatched it and stuck it in his teeth.

They stood staring at each other with thong and rose between their teeth. Both burst out laughing, tossing rose and thong aside.

Riley lifted her dress and bunching it behind her, she hopped up on Killian and wrapped her legs around his waist. "Give me some Irish Thunder," she purred, proud of her newfound bravado to boldly ask for what she wanted.

"I'll give you more than that, Mrs. O'Sullivan." He backed her up to a stone wall and lifted his kilt. It took some comical maneuvering to line up their body parts, and both laughed at their hasty fumblings. "No worries, I've got this." Killian grinned while Riley squealed with delight.

When he slid inside of her, she moaned his name repeatedly, keeping time to his rhythmic thrusts. Killian uttered a slew of Irish that intensified Riley's fervor, making love for the first time as husband and wife—on top of a castle, no less.

After they peaked, smothering each other with post-coital kisses, Killian held her until their breathing slowed.

"Ahoy up there!" Declan's voice rang up to them. "Mr. and Mrs. O'Sullivan? Get down here, your fans are waiting!"

"Coming!" Riley and Killian responded, laughing at the timing of their pun-intended response.

Killian lowered her to the stone floor, and she stood admiring her new husband.

"Our first quickie on a castle top," she said breathlessly.

"Trust me, there'll be more, my warrior princess," said Killian, straightening his kilt.

Riley smoothed out her dress. "We'll do this again in another three thousand years."

He shot her a devastatingly irresistible grin. "Gives us something to look forward to."

"Sure does." Riley winked and gathered her wedding gown to descend the seventy-six steps. Dizzy with happiness, gratitude, and everything else that goes with dreams coming true, she made her careful journey down the spiral staircase. With each step, Riley realized she'd learned a few things—like the importance of asking for what she wanted—and taking the necessary risks to get it. That one singular paradigm shift had changed her life.

Zippy was right. Her advice to Riley of not allowing fear stand in the way of her happiness changed everything and letting go of judgment had opened her heart to unlimited possibility. Like falling in love with an Irish musician. She chuckled at the cliché: *American woman falls for an Irishman when he sings his way into her heart.*

Only this cliché had a twist. This Irishman had not only sung but he'd stripped his way into her heart. She found the one she'd been on a trajectory toward, spanning countless lifetimes. And he had found her. A bonding of the souls.

Taking the risk to love Killian—to truly love him— took courage on Riley's part. But it took even more courage to allow him to love her in return.

Killian was no longer a dream. But he would forever be her jungle man—the jungle man from Chacchoben.

Thank you for purchasing
this publication of The Wild Rose Press, Inc.

For questions or more information
contact us at
info@thewildrosepress.com.

The Wild Rose Press, Inc.
www.thewildrosepress.com